To Laura
your friend
Brian

THE CONTINUING ADVENTURES OF A TIME TRAVELING HIPPIE SURFER

BRIAN S. JARVIS

Copyright © 2019 Brian S. Jarvis.

Photo: Billy Hill@g-townsurf
Cover Design: Cinn Roland
Editing by: Karen Albright
Author Photo: Susan Dumas

All rights reserved. No part of this book may be reproduced, stored, or transmitted by any means—whether auditory, graphic, mechanical, or electronic—without written permission of the author, except in the case of brief excerpts used in critical articles and reviews. Unauthorized reproduction of any part of this work is illegal and is punishable by law.

This is a work of fiction. All of the characters, names, incidents, organizations, and dialogue in this novel are either the products of the author's imagination or are used fictitiously.

ISBN: 978-1-4834-9433-3 (sc)
ISBN: 978-1-4834-9432-6 (e)

Because of the dynamic nature of the Internet, any web addresses or links contained in this book may have changed since publication and may no longer be valid. The views expressed in this work are solely those of the author and do not necessarily reflect the views of the publisher, and the publisher hereby disclaims any responsibility for them.

Any people depicted in stock imagery provided by Getty Images are models, and such images are being used for illustrative purposes only.
Certain stock imagery © Getty Images.

Lulu Publishing Services rev. date: 01/25/2019

Contents

CHAPTER 1 - STRANGER THAN FICTION	1
CHAPTER 2 - POE THE DOG AND SUBTERFUGE	7
CHAPTER 3 - DR. PEPPER ON MARS	11
CHAPTER 4 - THE RED PLANET	14
CHAPTER 5 - SURFING IN 1414	19
CHAPTER 6 - TOPSAIL.	23
CHAPTER 7 - HOW? AND HOW!	29
CHAPTER 8 - DUMBER THAN MUD ON A ROCK	38
CHAPTER 9 - DEATH BEFORE DISCO!	44
CHAPTER 10 - STAYIN ALIVE, STAYIN ALIVE!	49
CHAPTER 11 - HOT DOGS IN SPACE!	55
CHAPTER 12 - PLASTIC FANTASTIC LOVER!	59
CHAPTER 13 - DEATH TAKES A HOLIDAY.	65
CHAPTER 14 - BUT IT'S ALL OVER NOW.	69
CHAPTER 15 - GOING, GOING, GONE	74
CHAPTER 16 - THE BEAT GOES ON	82
CHAPTER 17 - GIMME SHELTER	85
CHAPTER 18 - NOT IN KANSAS ANYMORE.	90
CHAPTER 19 - HEARD IT THROUGH THE GRAPEVINE	93
CHAPTER 20 - TOTALLY DUDE!	99
CHAPTER 21 - SO WHAT DO YA THINK?	104
CHAPTER 22 - THEY WENT THAT AWAY……!	109
CHAPTER 23 - WHO'S ON FIRST?	114
CHAPTER 24 - "SAY A FEW SYLLABLES MOE!"	121
CHAPTER 25 - SAVE THAT THOUGHT	126
CHAPTER 26 - NAME THAT TUNE.	132
CHAPTER 27 - "THAT'S ALL FOLKS"	136
CHAPTER 28 - A SILVER LINING	141
CHAPTER 29 - WELL THAT COVERS THAT!	145
CHAPTER 30 - SAY WHAT?	149

Stranger than Fiction
Chapter 1

Time Travel is a stone cold fact. I'm waking up to my seventh day as a Time Traveler. It still seems like a dream, but it is not, it is very real. There is no place in all of time I cannot travel to and return.

Until a few days ago I had what could be called a normal life. Then I stumbled upon the "Dome of Time" and met the Keeper of Time, the Universe, and all Things, "Carl the First." From that moment on nothing in my life would ever be the same.

The Dome of Time has just been sitting in the North Carolina woods behind my house since before the beginning of time. I am the first person ever in all of time to find the Dome. I still have no idea why me.

This all happened really fast. I woke up on my 25th birthday as a normal human, and by the time I went to bed I had Time Traveled five times, gone through the "Dorian Gray" effect and would remain 25 years old for the next 500 plus years. Needless to say being 25 years old for the next 500 plus years would be noticed for sure, so I gave up my life as I knew it to be able to time travel. There is no regret in my decision.

I now live outside the normal life cycle in the Dome of Time with "Carl the first" and a time traveling surfer chick from California named Sandra. We two are the only human time travelers in the entire universe.

Sandra is a trip, she is a tall, tan, blonde surfer chick, who just happens to be one very sharp woman, plus she is a babe. Sandra is my friend, we surf together, I enjoy being with her, we are lovers.

Carl is the keeper of time and is immortal, he looks to be about my and Sandra's age, mid 20's. More or less he is teaching the art of time traveling to Sandra and me.

To help me give up my old life, Carl made up a story about me moving out to California to live with my new girl friend Sandra. A great story about how Sandra and I had met surfing fell madly in love and I was moving to the west coast to be with her. The funny part is I had not met Sandra at that point.

My actual disappearing was a snap; Carl came up with the idea to have a big "going away" party at my favorite bar. A huge party with a live band, free beer and as Carl likes to say "lots of debauching." It was a great party, a fantastic way to give up my old life.

Check this out, Carl owns a phone called the 'Time Phone", not to be confused with the 'Time Travel Phone." The time phone lets you call both the past and the future. You just look up the time code in an old "Yellow Pages," dial it in, and you can talk to anyone in anytime going back to the invention of the telephone. Dude you can dial in the year, month, day, even the minute and second you want to call.

I used the time phone to call everybody I knew and let them know I was leaving and about my "Going away party." I called everyone I could think of to invite them to the party, and had them invite all their friends too. We wanted a huge blow out of a party.

Using the Time phone I called them three weeks in their past and changed their futures, I made the calls about my moving and the party on October 6th 1974. The party was on the night of October 4th, two days before I made the calls. All the calls took me less than one hour "Dome Time" to make. Time Travel can be so weird. Dude I was in October 4th 1974 three times in four days, when I say weird I mean it.

I have gone back in time 65 million years and visited the dinosaurs with Carl. Sandra, Carl and I went to the moon to watch Neil Armstrong's first step on the lunar surface in 1969.

We watched three atomic bomb tests in the years 1946, 1954 and 1962. Hell we rode to the edge of space in the blast made by a hydrogen bomb named "Bravo" in the year 1954.

For fun we traveled 20 years into the future to catch the Rolling Stones live in 1994 at Mile High Stadium Denver, what a great show! I heard songs live in person that had not been written yet, that was totally amazing.

Sandra and I have time tripped twice back to Hawaii to the year 1111 to go surfing. What a dream come true, surfing in Hawaii 100 years before it was discovered by the Polynesians. Sandra and I are both long time surfers and we are going to teach Carl how to surf, or at least that is the plan.

You have to understand this is all still sinking in with me. Talking about it is helping me keep things in perspective.

On a darker note, my first time trip alone was back to June 6th 1944, to watch the D-Day landing. That was one horrible experience. Thank God, Carl had programmed me in for only a two minute stay; it felt a hell of a lot longer at the time.

We three time tripped to 1974 Baltimore then we went back 125 years to October 4th 1849, to the night Edgar Allan Poe was found unconscious in the gutter three days before he died on October 7th. That trip shook us up; it was gut wrenching to watch. We were there as the drugged Edgar Allan was pushed out of the back of a horse drawn wagon onto the wet cold cobble stones of Shakespeare Street and left to die.

We found a little black stray dog we named "Poe" in the precise spot they would find Edgar Allan Poe laying in the gutter. It was exactly 125 years later to the night they dumped Edgar Allan that we found the dog Poe.

Carl and Sandra have just zapped back to Baltimore in the time shield to 10:15 p.m. on October 4th 1974 to bring the lost dog Poe back to North Carolina to live in the Dome of Time with us.

They will be back in less than one minute. You can Time Travel for hours, days, or months, stay up to one year, and only be gone one minute in Dome Time.

When Carl and Sandra get back to the Dome from Baltimore we will own a time traveling dog. A little black dog whose tail looks like a question mark, with black spots on his tongue and pointed fox ears, is going to become a time traveling dog. *Why the hell not?*

I'm floating on a rubber air mat in a heated swimming pool drinking my morning coffee in the Dome of Time. A pool that had not been here two days ago. Carl can bend and change time and had the pool installed in less than one day by zapping the workers around in time. I have no idea how he does stuff like that, he just does. It's like no big deal to him.

Check this out; I can hear the Rolling Stone's recording sessions live as I'm floating here in the Time Dome. Live music from 1964, being recorded in the Chess Records studios. Live music from 2120 South Michigan Avenue in Chicago as it is happening ten years ago. Dude I can hear the Stones talking to each other in the studio. I am listening to them record the first takes of songs I grew up hearing on the radio. Man these songs are on LP's I got as Christmas gifts when I was in my early teens. I'm hearing live the original track of songs I know by heart. Man, The Dome of Time is truly an amazing place.

The Dome of Time has a yellow pole in its center; the "Time Pole." Every event that has taken place since the beginning of time to way past the end of time is in that yellow pole. The yellow pole also is the exact center of the universe.

Carl told me that "being the center of the universe is really important," something about being in balance but he did not say much more than that. I must admit the center of the universe sounds important.

Oh, I forgot. Carl's job is waiting through all of eternity to kick the Yellow Time Pole if it ever malfunctions.

No fooling, that's his job. Kick the Time Pole if it ever fucks up. After all, Carl *is* the "Keeper of Time" whatever the hell that means.

Anyway, that same yellow pole was glowing and putting out a bright light for me to follow on the day I found the Dome of Time. Carl told me it was the first time the Time Pole has glowed since the beginning of time.

He said that the Time Pole wanted me to find the Dome of Time for unknown reasons.

Carl also told me "Time Travel was my destiny."

Damn I never knew I had a destiny before he told me I did, amazing!

The "Time Travel Phone" is a 1940's era dial phone sitting on an old phone company spool that Carl uses as a table. The phone is connected by a wire to the Yellow Time pole and that allows us to time travel. All you have to do is dial in the right number and there you are. There is an old gray note book, called the "Book of Time" with all the numbers of time in it. Just look up where you want to go, the time you want to be there, dial in the number, hang up and poof there you are.

Now this is a major bonus! Carl owns an old metal Igloo cooler that never runs out of Coors beer. The empty Coors cans continually recycle into new full unopened cans of Coors and end up back in the "Endless Cooler." No shit, they refill themselves, Carl told me he has no idea how they do it they just do. The Endless Cooler was a gift from these little 4 foot tall space traveling fish people called "the Norsins."

Norsins import tons of Coors from Golden Colorado, millions and millions of miles to their planet in huge refrigerated spaceships. Of course the Coors Brewery is in on it; selling tons of Beer to space traveling fish people is very profitable.

Turns out that one of their spaceships broke down and the Time Pole, being the center of the universe attracted them here. They hung out with Carl in the Dome of Time working on their ship for a few of days and gave Carl the Endless Cooler as a gift. The cooler follows Carl around and it is amphibious, it can swim. Dude that cooler never runs out of Coors, like *never*. I have become very fond of that cooler.

The Norsins loved to eat Big Macs, which Carl would supply to them by the dozens. Imagine walking into McDonalds 5 or 6 times in a few days and ordering 8 dozen Big Macs to go.

"I would like 8 dozen Big Macs to go please, no nothing to drink." He said the people working at the MacDonald started looking at him real funny. Carl told them his doctor had him on a Big Mac diet. That explanation seemed to make sense to the employees; one guy even asked him how his diet was going.

Norsins like to smoke hash, and drink lots and lots of Coors. They told Carl "they don't drink water, because fish have sex in it" a 'W.C. Fields' joke coming from the mouths of little beer drinking space traveling fish people. Carl said they told that same stale joke over and over and over and over and it always cracked them up. He said fish people sound like they are blowing bubbles when they laugh. *Why the hell not?*

He also told me smoking hash with a fish was a very strange experience, as I shake my head in disbelief.

The endless cooler is the older pre pop top model, but as Carl says it works great, so having to use a can opener is not a big deal. I do love that cooler.

Confusing enough? *Truth is stranger than fiction!* Dude this is just the beginning, I have 500 plus more years of time traveling ahead of me. I'm still trying to make sense of the last six days.

Dude let me explain the Dorian Gray Effect. Once you begin to time travel you stop aging and remain as old as the day you started to time travel; and you might live 500 years or more.

When you are "Dorianed" you are stronger and faster than you have ever been. You will never get sick again, your hearing, eye sight and sense of smell are incredible.

Check this out, one of the major advantages of the Dorian Effect is an unbelievable tolerance for alcohol; no fooling you can drink all day long and never get drunk, or hung over. As Carl puts it, maintain a great buzz but you are always under control.

Because of the Dorian Effect, once a person starts to Time Travel they have to cut all ties with their old life.

Being 25 yrs old for 500 plus years will be noticed for sure. So you become, to quote George Orwell, an "Unperson." I have been an unperson for six days and I do not miss my old life at all. I could hear the Rolling Stones in the background recording live.

"Time, Time, Time, is on my side yes it is; you always said you wanted to be free."

It is still sinking in that I'm a Time Traveler, and Time is on my side. Man I have grown to love that song.

Poe the Dog and Subterfuge
Chapter 2

Carl and Sandra just got back to the Dome with the little black dog we named Poe. "Hey guys I said, I see you found Poe."

"Yea, he was still laying in the street on October 4th 1974 where we left him when we zapped back to 1849. He was glad to see us" replied Sandra.

I got out of the pool dried off and walked towards the time pole. It is always 76 degrees in the Dome of Time, it feels wonderful.

Sandra was on one knee petting the dog telling him everything was fine, he was home now. As I got nearer I could see the poor dog was freaked by all this. He had gone from being lost and laying in the gutter on a foggy Baltimore night and was now in the bright light of day in North Carolina in a blink of an eye. He was standing on grass maybe for the first time in his life. Sandra was petting his shaking body telling him he was home now and everything would be fine.

Carl said "I will get something for him to eat" as he walked up to the house.

"You want something to eat Poe?" asked Sandra. In no time Carl was back with a bowl of left over's from the fridge, he set it down in front of Poe.

God knows the last time the poor dog had eaten; he inhaled the food with his tail wagging 100 miles an hour.

"Carl can you bring him some water please?"

"Sure thing Sandra" he said and went back to the house. He returned with a large glass bowl full of water. Poe was as thirsty as he was hungry and lapped up half the bowl of water in no time. His shaking had stopped and he was walking around sniffing everything with a wagging tail.

You could tell he was going to be Sandra's dog.

"Carl, going back to get Poe the dog was a very nice thing to do. I am sure you saved his life," smiled Sandra.

"It was your idea to adopt him said Carl; you have a big heart Sandra. You always amaze me." he said flashing his big Cheshire cat grin.

Poe was pressed right up next to Sandra's leg, his tail still wagging like mad. "Come on Poe she said let's take a walk." She started walking toward the pool on the dark green thick grass of the Time Dome. If dogs can smile Poe definitely had a big grin on his face.

Carl and I sat down in our lawn chairs by the yellow Time Pole, he reached into the endless Coors cooler and opened two Coors, handing me one. We watched Sandra and Poe the dog playing in the grass.

"The family keeps growing Carl; we now own a Time Traveling dog. *Why the hell not?* I remarked, it's no weirder than anything else in our lives."

"Hey Brian, Sandra has to make a few calls on the time phone and get Poe to the vets, she has to buzz to the pet store and pick up dog food, a collar, dog bed and other such items. She will time zap around in one of our trucks. While she is gone I was thinking about pulling a huge prank on the world. Sandra would be real pissed and try to stop us if she knew about this, so not a word to her. How about it Brian, are you in?" Carl was on a roll!

"It depends on what you have in mind, pulling a huge prank on the whole world sounds kind of intense. Carl you just love fucking around in time don't you? Man you are hopeless."

"You are right Brian, I'm hopeless, but I have all the time in the world to get that way." He said grinning.

"So what is your plan Carl?" We looked up to see where Sandra was, and make sure she could not hear what we were talking about.

Sandra and Poe were running in the grass together, on the far side of the Time Dome. Damn that little black Poe was one fast dog; he was running circles around her. Sandra sat down on the grass out of breath and Poe jumped on her, she lay flat on her back laughing like crazy with a 50 pound dog on top of her licking her face and wagging his tail. "Looks like love, said Carl, I like that dog, he is one smart dog."

"So Carl what's your plan man?"

"Check this out Brian, I want to go to Mars in the year 2016 and leave an empty Dr. Pepper bottle where the Mars Rover Curiosity will find it. The Rover Curiosity is crawling around Mars lifting up rocks looking for life. Yoo Hoo, life where are you? Hello there rocks are you alive?"

"Dude, that is so boring. We can spice things up a bit. Let's blow NASA's collective mind. We will leave an empty Dr.Pepper bottle right in the Rover's path. Not just any Dr Pepper bottle, but one of the old glass 1950's bottles; you know the ones with 10, 2 and 4 on them. I have one that is all faded out, one of the long neck ones, the 2 cent deposit kind."

"So what do ya think Brian, sound like fun, going to Mars and fuck with the world's mind? Just going to Mars will be a gas, fucking with the minds of the best and brightest is always a ton of fun," said Carl with a huge grin.

"We can zap to Mars in the time shield, drink Coors smoke hash and play Rolling Stone's tapes, best part is we will be gone less than one minute Dome time and Sandra will never know."

"Think about the shock factor to NASA. Right now they are creeping along looking for micro bacteria life forms and poof out of nowhere there is an empty Dr. Pepper bottle right in front of their faces. You know this would never make the news. The world could not handle it."

I can see the headlines: "There is Life on Mars and it Drinks Dr. Pepper! Man we can leave an old Rolling Stone's eight track tape next to the Dr. Pepper bottle. There is Life on Mars and they are Rolling Stones Fans!"

By now Carl was laughing so hard he had tears in his eyes. "Lots of drama, I love drama he said still laughing. Come on Brian it will be our little secret."

"Damn Carl, how do you come up with this stuff?"I asked him.

"Brian I have had all the time in the world to become a fuck up!"

Poe the dog came zipping by us, ran around our lawn chairs and the time pole, turned, jumped up and put his paws on my lap and started licking my face, his tail wagging as fast as it could go. I started petting his shiny black coat, telling him he is a "good dog". I got to admit I like this dog a lot.

Sandra walked up still out of breath, "What a great little dog, I see he likes you Brian."

"Okay what are you two up to? I can tell by the look on your faces, that you guys are up to something, you both have that got caught peaking in the woman's shower room look. You two are such little boys." She stated in a firm voice, while looking right at us.

"Sandra, why would you say that?" asked Carl.

"You are the worst liar, Carl your eyes give you away." she said.

"Who me?" responded Carl.

"Carl, you are such a damn juvenile delinquent, I know you two are up to something."

"Us up to something Sandra?" Carl was doing his best I'm innocent look. "You two are hopeless" she said with a grin.

"Looky guys I have to take Poe to the vet, and pick up some stuff at the pet store. I am going to use your pickup truck Brian. I like that little Toyota. I will time zap the truck around to get this all done. I'm going in to use the time phone and set this up, take a shower and get going."

"I have to make an appointment to see a local Doctor; I need to get my birth control pills prescription refilled. My prescription is from a doctor in California, I need one from a local doctor. Last thing we need is a Baby Time Traveler," said Sandra with a flip of her long blonde hair.

"WOW." "I never thought about the possibility of you guys having a baby. That would be one very strange kid, born to two Time Travelers. This is totally unreal, a Time Traveling baby? Damn, I don't think I could handle that. What if you had twins Sandra? This is damn scary!" Carl said, shaking his head.

"By all means Sandra please refill that prescription and soon. I have to think this one over. This is deep." said Carl.

"Yea, Carl I thought that would blow your mind," said Sandra looking Carl right in the eyes.

"I'm going to get cleaned up, hit the Doctors, drug store, and pet store, get Poe and then go to the vet."

"Come on Poe lets go check out your new home, she said and they started walking up to the house. You two guys behave yourselves while I'm gone, understand?"

"How the hell did Sandra know we were up to no good?" I said to Carl. "I told you Brian, Sandra always amazes me."

"Damn a time traveling kid that is sooooo freaky," said Carl, still shaking his head.

Dr. Pepper on Mars
Chapter 3

"Dude, asked Carl, what do ya think, do you want to zap up to Mars and blow some minds? As soon as Sandra leaves we can take off and be back before she is wise to us."

"Carl, Sandra knows we are up to something, one look at us and she had us pegged."

"I don't like sneaking behind Sandra's back, but I know she would flip out if she knew about us leaving the Dr. Pepper bottle behind on Mars, and I really want to pull this off. This is an all time classic prank, it just has to happen," said a laughing Carl.

"Yeah, I don't like going behind Sandra's back either, but I'm with you Carl, we have to do this. After they find it we will tell her, okay?"

"I would not have it any other way, said Carl; we can't have secrets between the three of us." "Sure Carl let's go to Mars. What's the plan?"

"Okay Brian we have to buzz up to the year 2003 when Mar's orbit is closer to earth, then on to Mars. We will be traveling at light speed and it will still take about 3 or 4 minutes to get there. Even when Mars is nearest to the Earth it is 35 million miles away. We will be moving at 671 million miles an hour, light speed is a *rush* dude. It makes riding in an atomic bomb child's play, you will love it. As always we will bring the endless Coors cooler and some hash with us. You cannot go to Mars and not drink Coors and smoke hash. It's a rule."

"We are going to land on Mars in the year 2003 then zap up to the year 2016 and land in Gale Crater and place the Dr. Pepper bottle in the path of the Rover Curiosity. With the internet tracking it's every move I know exactly where it will be. Let's plant the bottle so it will be found on Halloween October 31 st, 2016, if you're going to blow minds may as well blow them all the way. This will be fun." Carl had a big grin.

He continued to explain, "Sandra has three or four stops in time to make, so we have a total of at least two minutes Dome Time till she is back. We will be traveling in the time shield so we will only be gone about one hour travel time, I will make sure we are gone less than one minute Dome Time,so we have plenty of time to get back before she knows we are gone."

"Now comes the hard part; looking innocent when Sandra comes down to the time pole to look up the numbers of the times she is going to travel to today. She is wise to us man, there is no fooling that woman. Carl said shaking his head, Sandra always amazes me."

"I am going to look up the numbers for Mars and lock them into my Zippo lighter before Sandra gets here."

Carl picked up the Book of Times and started turning pages. "Earlier I checked the location of the Rover on Sandra's Lap Top. He stopped turning pages and said, here it is" and started dialing in numbers. He dialed in the first few numbers, held the Zippo next to the phone and hung up. The second time he must have dialed about forty numbers held his Zippo lighter next to the phone and hung up. Then he dialed forty more numbers, held his Zippo next to the phone again and hung up for the third time. "Got them he said. As soon as Sandra leaves we go to Mars."

"I'm going up to get the Dr. Pepper bottle out of my bed room and hide it so she won't see it. I will be right back. I love subterfuge." Grinned Carl.

No sooner did Carl get back with the old Dr. Pepper bottle then Sandra and Poe came out of the house and walked towards the Time pole. She had showered and changed her clothes. Sandra had on a sun dress; I almost fell out of my chair. She looked stunning as she walked towards us, but then again Sandra always looks great.

"Wow, you look fantastic babe. I have never seen you in a dress."

"Thank you Brian you are so sweet." She sat down in her lawn chair with Poe by her side, she told Poe to sit and he did. "What a good boy, you are so smart Poe." Sandra reached over and petted his head.

Sandra picked up the Book of Times and started looking up the Time numbers she needed and locking them into her cell phone. She looked up at

Carl and me and said, "you two are up to something, just don't get into any trouble, ya hear me guys." she said, with a flick of her hair.

"Here are my plans guys. I'm going to my doctor's appointment, get my prescription for birth control pills, buzz over to a drug store and get that filled. Then zap over to the pet shop and get what I need for Poe, then come back and pick up Poe and off to the vets we go."

"I will see you two children in a few minutes. I know Time Travel makes it so easy for you two to fuck up, and fuck up you will. Be careful, I will see you guys in a little while. She leaned over kissed me and said; I love the color of your hair Brian. You two play safe."

"I'm going to leave Poe here during my first two trips. She said you stay Poe, keep an eye on these two idiots."

"See you guys soon." She turned and walked toward the house. No sooner did the screen door close that Carl said, *"Time to go to Mars dude."*

The Red Planet
Chapter 4

"Hi, Ho, Hi, Ho it's off to Mars we go," exclaimed Carl.

"Crap I left the hash and the pipe in the house on the kitchen table. We cannot go to Mars without hash; I will be right back," said Carl as he got up and trotted towards the house. Carl is on one of his rolls.

Man, I said to myself, I'm going to Mars to fuck with the world's mind, and I can't help but grin. Dr. Pepper on Mars, only Carl could come up with that, it is the mother of all pranks. *Why the hell not?* Carl is right; Time Traveling is a lot of fun.

It took no time for Carl to get back with the pipe and the hash. He had a cassette tape in his hand, "can't go to Mars and not listen to the Rolling Stones it's a rule."

"You ready to go Brian? Light speed is the rush of all rushes. Drama, lots of drama, I just love drama" said Carl with that damn grin on his face.

"Carl, what about Poe? We can't take him with us, he could freakout."

"Don't worry about Poe, he is sleeping in the grass, I doubt he will know we are gone, we will be gone less than a minute."

"Okay here's the plan we are going to zap up to April 27, 2003 when Mars is closer to earth and take off from there to Mars and be back before Sandra gets home," Carl explained.

"Don't forget Brian you have to make a point of not being in the Time Dome on that date and time in the future. Rule Number One, you cannot run into yourself."

"Carl I will write it down for sure I said. We will make a point for me not to be here on April 27, 2003 dude."

"Good thinking." He grinned.

"Okay, next stop right here 29 years in the future." Carl took out his Zippo lighter clicked it twice, we heard the sound like having your head out the window of a speeding car and there we were looking at our house 29 years in the future.

"Remind me to get the house painted in 29 years Brian." What the hell can I say to a statement like that?

"Here we go Brian we are on our way to Mars, it will take about 3 minutes and 30 seconds to get there at light speed and I have the perfect song to play that happens to last just that long."

Carl clicked his Zippo lighter twice and we were off to Mars. I could hear the roar of the wind sound and it got dark immediately, with blurs of light flying by at an unbelievable rate of speed. I could see a red speck getting larger with every second, it was growing and glowing. Carl was sitting back in his lawn chair just grinning.

"Check this out." He plugged in the tape "Out of our Heads" by the Stones and the song "Spider and the Fly" started to play.

"I love this song," said Carl, he handed me a Coors and a glowing bowl of hash.

Dude you are on your way to Mars, I said to myself. You are smoking hash, drinking Coors and listening to the Stones rocking out at full blast. This is absolutely amazing and it's really happening, man I'm zipping through space at the speed of light.

The planet Mars is becoming more detailed every second, I can see a zillion shades of red, growing at an unbelievable speed. Man, I'm on my way to fucking Mars!

Carl started to sing along with the song, "she was common and flirty she looked about 30, I would have run away but I was on my own."

"Damn those boys can rock; Keith Richards can play the hell out of that guitar." He said. All I could do was look at Carl shake my head and say, "WOW!"

Mars is getting bigger fast, I mean really fast and yes it is red. I could see mountain ranges; I could make out craters of different sizes. I could see large expanses of red deserts and its famed canals. The planet was growing clearer with each second that passed.

The song ended and we were sitting a few feet above Mars, we stopped moving at the speed of light and came to a dead stop. There was no jerking, no jarring, we just stopped, and we went from light speed to floating over the surface of the red planet just like that. Poof we were on Mars! We sat floating in the silence of Mars, over whelmed by the sheer breath taking vastness of the untouched Red planet.

...*We are looking at what no other living soul has ever seen.*

The two of us could say nothing for the longest time.

"Dude is that the Rover?" I could see some kind of man made Lander thing just sitting there about twenty yards from us.

"Na, said Carl, that's the Viking Lander, it will get to Mars in July 1976, two years in the future in Dome time, twenty seven years ago in present Mar's time. I needed a point to zero in on, he replied. Now let's zap up to October 30, 2016, and to Gale Carter. Catch up with the rover Curiosity and plant our mystery bottle where Curiosity will find it on Halloween!"

"Woooooo..." He said in his best spooky sounding voice.

Carl took out his Zippo clicked it twice, I heard a brief wind sound and I was looking at the Mars rover, I could hear a buzzing sound as it moved. It had left tracks as it moved along; the only marks on the surface of the planet. The tracks looked like wounds.

The time shield can be moved, and Carl steered it forward about 25 yards. According to my calculation the Rover should be right about here tomorrow October 31. "This is where we plant the Dr. Pepper Bottle." He said in a serious voice.

He got on one knee, opened the hatch in the floor of the shield and stuck in the bottle. He sat down, and pushed a button by the tape player. The outside door of the hatch opened, the bottle fell a few feet, hit the surface on Mars and kicked up a small cloud of red dust. Some of the dust settled on the bottle. "Perfect Carl said, absolutely perfect, the dust is a nice touch. This calls for a bowl of hash and a Coors." He said as he handed me a Coors.

"I propose a toast, we stood up, touched our cans together, *the 1st Dr Pepper on Mars!"* Carl said. We took a big drink of ice cold Coors and we both started to laugh.

"This is going to blow some minds Carl, I can hear it now, Houston we have a problem!" I said. We both cracked up.

Carl then said. "Let's float around awhile and then buzz back to the Dome before Sandra gets home." He plugged in the tape again and "Play with Fire" started to play. "Don't play with me because you're playing with fire."

The vast emptiness of Mars was overwhelming; it looked like a desert, and everywhere there was drifting red sand. It was day light and we could see for miles and miles and miles.

We could see mountains with dozens of different shades of reds and dark shadows of black covering vast spaces of nothing but an untouched planet. My God I'm on Mars!

The Rover Curiosity looks so out of place, its tracks looked like scars on the pristine red surface.

The shield moved along floating a few yards above the Red planet. The music stopped, Carl and I said nothing as we floated in amazement above this planet named after the God of War. That red dot way off in the sky was now ten feet under us.

We are the first people on Mars and we littered. What a goof, I said to myself. My God I love Time Traveling.

For a short while we floated in silence exploring the red wonder called Mars. Carl looked at his Zippo. "We should be leaving, if we want to get back before Sandra does." He clicked the lighter six times and we were back at the Viking Lander, he clicked the Zippo six more times, I heard the wind and the blue dot that was earth started getting larger faster than fast.

Carl plugged in the tape again and "Satisfaction" started to play as we zipped at Light Speed through the vast nothingness of space. The song was still playing when we came to a stop back in the Dome of Time in the year 2003. Carl clicked his Zippo lighter six times and I heard the wind sound again and just like that we were sitting in the same place but we were back in 1974.

I looked over at Carl, "what a rush, I said shaking my head. Carl we just went to Mars. I went zapping through space at light speed, man I have got to calm down."

"Yea, we got to chill out, Sandra will be back real soon," said Carl. He opened two beers and handed me one.

I looked over and could see Poe laid out on the green grass still sound asleep. We had been to Mars and back and been gone less than one minute Dome Time.

"You know Brian, NASA will never admit they found that bottle. Maybe we should write them a letter asking for our 2 cents deposit back, send it postage due." He said. We both cracked up at the thought of that.

I could hear the Stones talking with each other in the background, then Mick counted "1, 2, 3" and the song "Good Times" started to play.

"There been good times, there been bad times, I've had my share of hard times too." Damn live Rolling Stones from 1964, got to love it, I said to myself with a real big smile.

We heard the screen door open and Sandra was walking toward us. "I see you guys are still sitting there drinking Coors, you guys are hopeless." She said.

"Hey Sandra we have been babysitting Poe." I replied.

As soon as the dog heard her voice he was wide wake and running up to her. She knelt down and petted him and told him he was a "good dog."

"I got my prescription filled and I picked up some great stuff for Poe, I never knew there were so many different kinds of dog food. That alone took forever. Looky Poe you have your own collar now, so you will never get lost again." She put a Tar Heel blue collar on him, his tail started to wag faster. "Nice choice of color there Sandra." said Carl. "I figured you would like that Carl."

"I came back to get Poe and take him to the vet for his check up and shots. I'm surprised you guys are here. I thought for sure you two would be out causing mischief."

"Who us Sandra? Mischief? What kind of mischief could we get into?" Carl was flashing that damn Cheshire cat grin of his.

Surfing in 1414
Chapter 5

"Hey Sandra, when you get back from the Vet do you want to go surfing? Asked Carl still grinning. You have never surfed in the Atlantic before have you? Brian surfs around here a lot and I'm sure he knows some great places to surf."

"Sure thing Carl lets go surfing said Sandra. Brian and I can start teaching you how to surf, we can take Poe with us. He would love going to the beach. This will be fun, I will be right back. Come on Poe we are going to take a ride in Time and visit the Vet. Then we will go to the beach. You want to go to the beach Poe?"

It was like that damn dog understood what Sandra was saying, he started wagging his tail and hopping around her in circles. "That is one goofy little dog." I said to Sandra.

"I will be right back." As she walked away she was singing, "Let's go surfing now everyone is learning how come on a safari with me."

"That woman loves to surf I said, too bad she can't sing." Carl and I both chuckled, but not too loud.

"Going surfing here in North Carolina is a great idea Carl. I know some great surf spots. I can bring a board for you and I think I have a pair of Birdwell trunks that will fit you, Tar Heel blue of course. Time you learned how to surf Carl. I have just the board to teach you on. It can get crowded here sometimes and it is mid October the water is starting to chill down." I said.

"We can Time Travel back to the first week in September when the water is warmer or we can travel back in Time to before anyone ever surfed in

North Carolina. Wow we will be the first people to surf in North Carolina, this is so cool."

"Carl we can Time zap back in your 4x4 truck, it has more room than mine. We will bring the endless Coors cooler and pack a big lunch. We can drive around on the beach, till we find the break we want to surf."

"Bring Poe with us that will make Sandra happy. I still feel bad about sneaking off to Mars behind her back, but leaving that bottle behind is such a great prank, we had to do it. I said. Taking Sandra surfing in the Atlantic is our way of making it up to her."

"Cool, let's get ourselves together before she gets back. Carl look up North Topsail beach, it's a left and right break. Topsail is a barrier island not too far from here, a real nice beach, clear water. There are a bunch of vacation homes on the island, more every year, but I doubt they will be there in the past. Having the place to ourselves will be different. Lock the number into your Zippo Carl and we are all set."

"What year you want to go back to?" asked Carl.

"How about September 1 1414, that sound like a cool year, what do ya think Carl?"

"September 1 1414 sounds cool to me," grinned Carl. Hey Brian you know there is a chance we will run into the local tribe of Indians, the "Cape Fear" tribe. They had a village about 20 miles up the Cape Fear River; I think it was called "Necoes." It would not have been too far from the Dome of Time."

"Not much is known about the Cape Fear Indians. I do know that they went to war in 1667 with the British settlers; I think the British were trying to enslave some of their tribe. That would piss me off too," said Carl.

"By the early 1800's the whole tribe had been wiped out by smallpox and wars. I just love civilization." Said Carl, shaking his head.

"If the Cape Fear Indians do come across us I'm not sure how we will be greeted. They would have never seen pale skin people before us. I have found over my years of time travel, that blue eyes always fascinate primitive dark eyed people. Wait till they see Sandra's green eyes that will really get their attention. Hell, just wait till they see Sandra period, tall blonde women are hard to come by in 1414 North Carolina."

"Carl what happens if they are hostile? Should we bring our guns?"

"Na Brian I don't want to shoot anyone, besides they would not know what the hell a rifle is to begin with. If things get bad we can always zap out of there. Not to worry Brian, if they are hostiles, I found that by cranking up the stereo in the truck and playing "Purple Haze" by Jimi Hendrix at full volume is enough to scare any hostiles away. They don't hear a lot of Hendrix in the year 1414." said a laughing Carl.

"That reminds me, he said still grinning, we can Time Trip back and catch Jimi live sometime, seeing Jimi again would be fun. Dude I hung out with him back in the day. He is one trippy dude. The way I see it you are allowed to be that off the wall if you can play guitar like he could."

"Wow let's go to see Jimi Hendrix for sure dude, I would love to meet Jimi and see him playing live, dude a dream come true." I said to Carl. "Yeah, Brian we will make a point of dropping in on Jimi, it will be fun, I like the guy, and he always has great smoke."

"Anyway let's get back to dealing with the natives, I do enjoy interacting with friendly locals said Carl, it is always interesting, I always learn a lot from them. Turning them on to ice cold Coors is always fun. They have never seen anything like a cold Coors. M&Ms are big with primitive people. M&Ms always puts a big smile on their faces. I have some stashed just for trips like this."

"With our translator rings we can talk to them."

"It is always a freak out to the natives that we can speak and understand their language. Here's when that Demi God thing I told you about comes in to play Brian, we always have to be careful not to fuck with these people's heads." Seeing a pickup truck for the first time, along with pale skinned people with blonde and red hair, can blow their minds right off. If they see us riding waves it would look like we are walking on water to them."

"We got to be careful if we run across these people. I want to be friends and not worry about them shooting arrows at us. Lots of drama, I just *love* drama." said Carl, with a sparkle in his eyes.

"Let's pack a big lunch and stick three surfboards in the truck. The endless cooler will jump in by itself. I will lock the number for Topsail into the Zippo. As soon as Sandra gets back with Poe we are going surfing in the year 1414" said a grinning Carl.

He leaned over, and picked up the old gray notebook. Thumbed through it, said "I found it" and dialed in about 20 numbers, held his Zippo next to the phone and hung up. "Let's load up my truck, this will be fun." He said.

We got up, walked up to the house and went into the kitchen. Carl started packing a bunch of left over southern fried chicken and cheese in the picnic cooler for our lunch. We put in about a dozen bottles of Dr. Pepper, and of course the M&M's. We packed the cooler full of ice and off we went.

We went out the Dome's garage and opened the doors. Carl pulled his truck up about ten feet so we could get the boards in the back. He stuck the picnic cooler in the bed, and sure enough the endless Coors cooler was sitting there waiting on us. Carl leaned over, patted the top of the endless cooler and said "good endless cooler." He looked at me and had that damn grin on his face again.

Man I said to myself, how the hell does that cooler move around by itself? No matter, I love that damn cooler!

I went into my bedroom and found a pair of baggies that would fit Carl, by the time I got back, my truck was sitting back in the garage and Sandra was standing there with Poe the dog talking to Carl. "Hey babe, how did the vet trip go?" I asked.

"Poe is in real good shape, no worms or the like, a little under weight, he got his shots and I picked up heart worm pills and stuff to keep fleas off him. Poe got a shampoo, he was filthy. The Vet said as near as he can tell Poe is just over a year old. He liked the fact we took in a stray dog. Poe time traveled in the truck like he has been doing it all his life, he is such a smart dog Sandra said. She bent over and petted his head; you're a real good boy Poe." Damn that dog loves Sandra. "That's great news about Poe." I said.

"Sandra, we are going surfing right now. Grab your bathing suit, we packed a lunch and we are bringing the endless cooler, and the hash. I stuck a board in the truck for you and we are bringing Poe with us. Crap we forgot our lawn chairs; I will get them."

"Sandra we are going Surfing in the year 1414. Carl told me we may run into some hostile Indians, but worry not, because we are packing M&Ms and Jimi Hendrix."

Sandra just stood there looking at me with a puzzled look on her face. "M&M's and Jimi Hendrix Brian?"

Topsail.
Chapter 6

"Hey guys hurry up; it's almost 9:00 a.m. Dome Time. I want to go surfing" I yelled as I walked into the kitchen.

Carl came walking into the kitchen, "Brian these trunks fit me great, thanks man." One look at his pale white legs and I had to chuckle, "nice tan you got there Carl."

"You like that?" he asked. Sandra walked in and started to laugh. "Great legs Carl." she said.

"Hey Brian, will you tie up my top? I hate these things." she said, holding the top pressed to her chest. Poe has become her shadow and was right beside her as she walked over to me she turned so I could tie up her bathing suit top.

"Good thing I have some Bull frog sun screen; Carl you are going to need it for sure. Nothing worse than a sunburned Keeper of Time, the Universe and all Things, she said cracking up. Sorry Carl but your legs are so fricking white, in millions of years you never bothered to get a tan?"

"I had a nice tan when I was living in ancient Rome, wearing togas will do that. Lying out in the sun to turn brown has never crossed my mind before today Sandra."

"Tans are a byproduct of surfing. We have a pool now Carl, I would strongly recommend you start working on a tan if you are going to take up surfing."

"Come on you guys let's get going, the truck is loaded, are you guys all set?" I asked. Both of them said "let's go."

"We will level 3 back so if we do run into anyone they will not remember us after we leave. Push the green button on your time travel watches you guys." said Carl.

"I have got the number in my Zippo, next stop September 1 1414, Topsail beach North Carolina."

We walked out to the Dome's garage and got into Carl's 4 by 4 Chevy pickup. Sandra in the middle, then I got in, and ended up with a little black dog sitting on my lap with his front feet on the door, looking out the rolled down passenger's side window.

"This is real comfy, I have a dog in my face Sandra, Poe is one goofy ass dog." I said as he licked my face.

Carl took out his Zippo, clicked it twice, and we could hear the wind sound for a few seconds as light flew by us in an amazing blur. Then we stopped, there was the Atlantic right in front of us, just like that we were sitting on a deserted pristine beach, watching some real pretty 2 and 3 foot waves breaking a few dozen yards away.

"My God; Carl this beach is about 100 yards wider than it is in 1974."

"That's because Global Warming has not yet started in 1414 Brian," he replied.

"You said something about that before Carl, what the fuck is global warming?" I asked. "I will fill you in about global warming in awhile Brian; it is too damn depressing to talk about now."

"Carl yesterday you said I would get a kick out of Global Warming, now you say it's too depressing to talk about, what's up with that dude?" I asked.

"Later Brian I will explain everything, but now let's just enjoy being at the beach in the year 1414, okay?"

Carl started the truck, "Lets drive down the beach a ways and explore he said. We will talk later, I promise dude."

I cannot even begin to explain the rush of being the first people ever to drive along the virgin North Carolina beach. The water was a crystal clear blue; the sand was pure clean drifted dunes.

Not one sign of humans, no beach houses to be seen. There is no plastic, no foam cups, no abandoned kid's toys, no cigarette butts, and no manmade crap at all littering the beach. Not a foot print in sight, this beach has looked like this for 1000's of years, untouched.

"By the time I surf here 560 years from now, all this is gone for good." I said.

We drove down the beach very slowly parallel to the water, under but a light blue cloudless sky, or as Carl would say a "Tar Heel Blue" sky. Not a cloud in sight, a pretty little shore break running the length of the beach.

"Damn, Carl all of my landmarks are gone and the break is different than when I surf here in 500 plus years. Right up there looks like a good spot, there is a little peak of land sticking out into the ocean, let's go out there." I said.

We drove up to the little sand bar and parked the truck. No sooner did I get the door open than Poe took a flying leap out onto the beach. Sandra followed me out, and said "My God guys this is totally unbelievable. Smell this air; it is so clean, unreal. I love this." she said.

Poe was running and sniffing everything, he is one fast little dog, you could tell he was having a blast. Earlier today he was lost in the night and laying in the gutter in 1974 Baltimore, now later in the same day he was running in the bright sun on a clean beach in the year 1414. "Look at him go said Sandra, man he is having fun."

"Look Babe I said why you don't paddle out and catch a few waves. After all this is your first time in the Atlantic Ocean, you may as well be the first person to ever surf in North Carolina, hell woman you will be the first person ever to surf on the east coast period."

"Wow Brian this will be so cool; a California surfer girl will be the first person to go surfing on the east coast."

"Sandra, I don't think it will end up in the history books babe."

She laughed, put her arms around me and kissed me.

"I will keep an eye on Poe; I'm going to start Carl's surfing lesson. Go have fun babe." I said.

She picked up her board and started walking toward the clear blue ocean. "Brian this is so outstanding." she said, as she started to run toward the water, I grabbed Poe's collar, she dove in on top of her board and started to paddle out. She paddled out about 30 yards sat up turned her board, paddled for the first wave to come in and caught it, cranked a hard left turn, tucked into the pretty little tube and rode a ways, she kicked out yelling, "I love this."

"I told you Sandra is a great surfer Carl; you have your work cut out for you dude. Let's get started."

"Carl it just hit me, a little while ago you and I were floating around above Mars, pulling off a huge joke on the world. Now less than an hour later dome time we are going to be floating around in the Atlantic, 78 years before Columbus discovers the New World."

"Brian we can pull off one more joke on the whole damn world again, Carl said. We can have some real fun and be waiting on the beach in 1492 when Columbus lands and welcome him to India. Hello there Columbus, welcome to India. Hey how about a can of cold Coors after your long voyage Christopher?"

"That would blow his age of enlightenment mind running into you, me and Sandra, standing on the beach, waving and holding a big sign, "Welcome to India Chris. Yep Chris you did it, you discovered a sea route to India!

Do you want to buy some madras shirts Chris? How about a sari for Queen Isabella?"

I looked at a grinning Carl and said, "How the hell do you come up with this stuff dude?"

"I have had all the time in the world to become a major fuck up Brian." he was still grinning.

"Come on Carl let's get started teaching you how to surf." I took my 10 foot board out of the truck and laid it on the sand. I went over the parts of the board, I showed him how to paddle, how to wipe out, and I demonstrated how to do the "Pop -Up." I made him do a dozen pop -ups on the beach.

We had a long rope with us and tied Poe up to the bumper of the truck; we put down the tail gate so he had plenty of shade and left him a bowl of water. I turned to Carl and started singing "let's go surfing now everyone is learning how come on a safari with me."

"Brian, never make fun of Sandra's singing again, you can't carry a tune in a bucket he said laughing. Okay let's get on with this." he said.

"Carl I'm going to be standing next to you in the water holding the board. I will get you in trim on the board and push you into an easy wave, when I yell NOW, you try to get up. Okay you ready Carl?"

"Let's do this dude." He said.

We walked out to about waist deep water, I helped Carl get centered on the board, said "here we go dude." I saw a 2 foot wall of white water coming toward us I pushed the board into the wave riding with my weight on the tail to keep the nose up, and yelled NOW! Damned if Carl did not get up his first try and ride right up to the beach.

I could hear Sandra yelling "Way to go Carl. That was really good dude, you are surfing."

"I told you I would be out surfing you two in no time he said with a big grin, that was a lot of fun."

"Ready to try again? This time I want you to paddle into the wave yourself without me pushing you. When I yell now, get up again. Okay Carl here we go." I waited till the white water was about a board length away and yelled "paddle"; he caught the wave by himself. I yelled "NOW" and he got up, rode about 20 feet and fell off. "Not bad dude I said, let's try it again."

The second time he paddled into a wave he got a nice ride right up to the beach. I body surfed a wave up to the beach and joined him. "Okay here's what I want you to do, go out till you are standing in waist deep water. Wait till you see the wave coming, jump on the board, and paddle till you feel it pushing you, then get up. Just keep doing that for awhile and I will take you up a notch when you get that part down. I'm going to grab my board and go surfing with Sandra." I told him.

"Hey Brian thanks, I appreciate you taking the time to teach me how to surf, this is so much fun, I love it!"

"Carl one thing we have a lot of is Time, wait till you get my bill, be careful," I said as I grabbed my board and paddled out to surf with Sandra.

It took no time for me to get out to Sandra; I sat up on my board next to her. "Carl is doing great she said, it will be fun having him to surf with; I noticed he is a goofy foot too. I see a lot of lefts breaks in our future." she said.

"Brian can you believe this, we are surfing in the year 1414. We can Travel in Time, Brian this is unbelievable, but it's happening, welcome to our new lives. Brian we are Time Travelers." She sat on her board and stared into my eyes for a few seconds; she turned and paddled into a wave. My God Sandra is right! We are Time Travelers, damn Brian this is real. I said to myself. *Why the hell not?*

Sandra and I traded wave after wave for about two hours, we kept an eye on Carl, and he was coming along nicely.

"What do you think we grab some lunch?" She asked. We both caught the same wave and rode up to Carl and Sandra said "lunch time dude, catch a wave in."

"We all rode the same wave in, walked up the beach, laid our boards down and started walking towards the truck and a sleeping Poe.

"So Carl what do you think about surfing?" Sandra asked as we walked back up to the truck. "I can see why you guys love to surf; I'm hooked." he said flashing that damn grin of his.

Poe was up and wagging his tail, Sandra let him off the leash. I pulled the lawn chairs off the truck bed and sat them by the pickup facing the ocean.

I grabbed the picnic cooler and sat it on the beach. The endless cooler was sitting next to Carl's chair. How the hell does that damn cooler move around like that? I asked myself again.

"You guys want a Coors?" Carl asked, we both said "for sure." We sat chit chatting about surfing and slowly eating our lunch and drinking Coors. We could not have planned a nicer day, it was warm, the sun was bright, not a sound besides the wind and the waves. Not a sign of mankind to be seen. Poe started a low growl.

Carl stood up looked over towards the mainland and said "don't look now boys and girls but we have company."

How? And How!
Chapter 7

"Carl, are they the Cape Fear Indians? They are beautiful looking people, look at that hair. They have women with them; look how young they all are. They can't be more than 20 years old." said Sandra.

We were standing on the Ocean side of Carl's pickup looking inland; this is the white man's first view of Native American Indians. There were three young men and two girls all in their late teens or early 20's, standing on a sand dune about twenty yards from us.

Sandra was right, these are magnificent looking people.

Dark trim body's, they stood straight, the men looked about 5 foot 7 or so, the two women were almost as tall.

They showed no fear of us, as they pointed at us and talked amongst themselves. They all wore loin cloths and necklaces made of shells. The women were bare breasted with about a dozen shell necklaces hanging over their boobs. They had unbelievable long black straight hair, tied back with a long strip of buckskin, with a few feathers tucked into the strip.

The men had leather bags with a bow and arrows hung over their shoulders and one had a rock tomahawk hanging from a long buckskin strap across his chest. All five of them had stone knives with wooden or bone handles in little leather cases, tucked in a buckskin belt tied around their waist.

"Carl what do we say to them? HOW?" Sandra asked.

"You have watched too many John Wayne movies. Sandra. How? Really Sandra? These will be the first words spoken by a white man to Native American Indians, I don't think "How" is appropriate.' said Carl.

"I think you're right, Sandra said; let's make it memorable, after all this is the first time our two different cultures have ever met."

Carl walked around the front of the pickup, still munching on a fried chicken leg; he waved at the Indians and said the now famous first words spoken by a white man to Native Americans.

"What's up Dudes?"

"Carl those are the words that will go down in history? I said shaking my head. What's up dudes? Carl you are a mess."

Without missing a beat Carl said, "I know I'm a mess but I have had all the time in the world to get that way."

"Hey Sandra, come around here and let them get a good look at you, females have a soothing effect on people. Come on over here next to me Sandra, smile and wave." he said. Sandra was holding Poe by his collar, he was no longer growling, and he stood there wagging his tail. Sandra walked around the truck and waved, and said "Hello, we are not from around here."

"Sandra I think they know you are not from around here, said Carl. You are such a goof Sandra."

She looked at him and replied in a low voice, "Carl if they scalp me I will kill you."

"Sandra, it was common practice to pay a bounty for Indian scalps, it continued right up to the 1890's." said Carl in almost a whisper.

"Show time boys and girls. I have the feeling this will be great, he said. We are going to have lunch with the Cape Fear Indians."

"Please come on over and join us and share our food." He said with a big grin on his face and motioned to the Indians with a wave of his arm.

All five of the Indians started to walk towards us and the light blue pickup truck. "Greetings, strange ones, said the oldest of the males. We are Waccamaw people, this is our tribal land, and you are welcome. You speak in our tongue strange ones."

"Yes we speak your language said Carl, please take part in our food." I came around the truck and stood next to Sandra. The young Indian girls showed no fear of us and walked right up to Sandra; the youngest one reached up slowly and touched Sandra's long blond hair. "Your hair is like the sun she said, very pretty." she started to giggle.

The other young girl got down on one knee and started to pet Poe. "He is a nice dog she said, I own a dog too, and my dog is a good hunter."

The girl who was standing nearest to Sandra said "My name is Wind Song and she is my friend Smiling Water."

"My name is Sandra, this is Brian, and the other is named Carl."

"The one named Brian has hair the color of sunsets said Wind Song. Carl has hair like the sun too. All of you have strange color eyes, your men have eyes like the sky, Sandra your eyes are the color of the shining trees."

"Wind Song you and Smiling Water both have very beautiful eyes and I love your hair said Sandra. Who are your friends Wind Song?"

"The men with us are my brothers Walking Bear, Leaping Fox and our friend Gray Wolf. We are fishing and hunting today, we come here often. We paddle down here in our canoe, the fishing is very good."

"We mean you no harm; you have many strange things of wonder we have never seen" said Wind Song.

Walking Bear slowly reached over and tapped Carl's truck, he pulled his hand away. "What is this big thing the color of the sky?" He asked. I have never felt anything so hard, what is it called?"

"We call it a pick-up truck, said Carl, it is a land canoe. I will take you all for a ride later, but first please share our food. We have Southern fried chicken, sharp cheeses, homemade beard, and Dr. Peppers, oh and M&Ms as a treat, said Carl, you are welcome to join us".

"These are things we know nothing about said Wind Song, are they foods?"

"Yes these are our foods, please come and join us. Try sitting in the lawn chair Wind Song." said Sandra.

Wind Song slowly sat in the chair, a big grin came over her face, "the lawn chair is strangely comfortable. One more wonder we know nothing about." Smiling Water sat on one of the other lawn chairs, the men sat on the sand. Sandra opened the picnic cooler, took out five bottles of Dr. Pepper, opened them, and handed one to each of our guests.

Walking Bear exclaimed "these are cold as winter, how can such a thing be?"

"Take a drink," Sandra said with a big grin. All 5 of the Indians put the cold bottles slowly to their mouths and took a small sip. Each one of them got a huge smile and took a big drink.

"These are the taste of joy I have never tasted before said Wind Song. These are Dr. Peppers?"

"Yes, Wind Song, we call them Dr. Peppers, try some Southern Fried Chicken. Sandra handed each one a chicken leg, these are a bird we grow just to eat".

They all took a small bite, the look on their faces was one of amazement;" these birds are a taste of wonder." said Wind Song.

"Eat up, we have plenty. Try these, we call them sharp cheddar cheese and bread, they too taste great." Sandra had this situation under control; she was a very gracious hostess.

I am sitting on Topsail beach in the year 1414 having lunch with five Native Americans. *Why the hell not?* I said to myself. I am digging every second of this. These are the nicest, easiest going, laid back, unspoiled people I have ever met. Their smiles were deep and contagious.

As we sat eating our lunch, Carl said "would you guys like to hear some music?"

"We make music on drums and sing songs and dance said Wind Song. We like our music, it is fun. I know nothing of your music. What is your music like?"

"It is a pleasant sound that floats on the air, we enjoy it a lot, explained Carl, with his damn grin. Let me plug in a tape for us to listen to." said Carl.

"What is a tape?" asked Wind Song. "A tape is a little box the music lives in." he said. Carl stood up leaned into the truck; I could not help but wonder how our quests would react to Rock and Roll. It will be in a language that they will not understand, and I'm sure they would never have heard anything like it before.

"Carl be careful said Sandra, I don't need you scaring the shit out of these people, with blaring Rock."

"I got it under control." he said. I was braced for the Rolling Stones to come blasting out of the stereo, much to my surprise, "Rhapsody in Blue" by George Gershwin started to play at a low volume. "Wow, Carl that's a very pleasant choice of music, I love Gershwin, said Sandra, nice pick Carl."

Looking over at our guests, I could tell they liked Gershwin too. They were looking around at the air, and their bodies started to sway with the music. "The sound flows in the air, it is pleasant to my ears." said Wind Song.

We had finished all the chicken and Sandra said, "I have a real treat for everyone; we call them M&Ms." She took out a plastic baggie full of M&Ms and poured a few in everyone's hand.

"These are food? Standing Bear asked, they look like hard strange colored berries."

"They are what we call a treat said Sandra, try them. Just put them in your mouth and bite into them, they are very good." The look on the faces of our Indian quests was priceless." M&Ms are most tasteful; they make the inside of my mouth smile. You can make sounds float in the air, you can make cold in the middle of the hot time, you have foods we have never dreamed of, you have lawn chairs to sit in, you own a land canoe. Your hair and eyes are such strange colors, you are people of wonder." Said Wind Song.

"We were worried you would be hostile and mean said Gray Wolf, so we watched you for a long time."

"They have a nice dog; I told you they could not be mean and own a dog this nice." said Smiling Water as she petted Poe.

That damn dog loves women, he is one smart critter.

"Sandra, Wind Song continued, before we saw you floating across the water on those strange little canoes, said Wind Song. Can you teach Smiling Water and me how to do such a thing? You danced in the waves. It was a thing of wonder to watch. You and the great water flowed as one."

"My God said Sandra. I have never heard surfing described with such pure feelings. Sure I would be happy to show you how to surf. Hey Brian, can you help me out here teaching these girls how to surf?"

"Sure thing Sandra, they are both small and in good shape this will be duck soup."

"Hey Carl, how about you taking Walking Bear, Gray Wolf, and Running Fox for a ride in our land canoe?"

"Yeah that sounds like fun." said Carl with that Cheshire cat grin again. "Brian and I are going to show the girls how to surf."

"Poe get inside the canoe with me, said Carl. Okay you guys get in the back of the canoe. Let's take a ride in our land canoe".

"But you have no paddles." said Running Fox.

"Don't worry dude, I have a 350 cubic inch engine, with 8 cylinders under the hood; we don't need no stinking paddles."

Carl got in and started the truck and very slowly started driving down the beach with Poe hanging out the passenger's side window. I noticed he had changed the tape to the Rolling Stones. I could hear "Love is love and not fade away," blasting out as he drove off.

Standing Bear, Running Fox and Gray Wolf were kneeling looking out of the truck bed grinning from ear to ear and waving at us. Poe was still standing with his head out the passenger side window. In no time, we could no longer see the truck.

"Okay Girls, both of you can swim right?" Asked Sandra. "We swim very well, we grew up swimming." said Smiling Water. "Okay take off your necklaces, knifes and feathers, tie your hair back." Sandra instructed.

The Indian girls had great boobs, these are two beautiful almost nude young women, this is not going to be easy I said to myself. It was like Sandra read my mind. She walked over to me and smiled; she leaned over and whispered in my ear, "Remember where you are sleeping tonight." As she poked me in my ribs.

My "who me look" was shot right down.

We went over some of the basics of surfing on the beach then we took the girls out in the white water and pushed them into waves, they both got up their first try.

In all my years of surfing I had never seen two chicks take to surfing so fast. They caught waves by themselves in no time; they even turned the boards, fricking remarkable. Their smiles were huge.

In about an hour Carl came driving back up way too fast, with the Rolling Stones blasting out at full volume. He kicked up a wall of flying sand as he turned hard, and came to a stop, much to the delight of his three passengers.

We had the girls ride one last wave to the beach. All five of our new friends ran to each other and started talking all at once.

"Carl, did you give those guys any Coors? They sure are wound up", said Sandra. "I just gave them one each, said Carl, they loved them. I turned them on to a few bowls of hash too."

"They flipped out over my Zippo lighter, it made their day. They called it a Fire box. Check this out, it turns out they smoke pot, they called it the Weed of Dreams."

"I like that Sandra said. Weed of dreams is too cool".

"I taught them some English. Okay boys what did you learn to say?" All three turned looked at Sandra and me and at one time started chanting.

"Jumping Jack Flash it's a gas, gas, gas!" they started laughing and dancing. "Jumping Jack Flash it's a gas, gas, gas." Gray Wolf was laughing so hard he fell down.

"Great, said Sandra, the only English they know is a Rolling Stone song, Carl you are hopeless."

"I know I'm hopeless Sandra, but I have all the time in the world to get this way." he said with his big grin.

"Wow Carl, we watched the Rolling Stones live playing that song a few yards in front of us in 1994 Denver. Carl that show is 580 years from now and we went to that show a few days ago! Time loves to fuck with your head." said Sandra.

"Yep, Time Travel is a gas, gas, gas!" Carl agreed still grinning.

All five of our guests were laughing, and singing Jumping Jack Flash it's a gas, gas, gas!

"Carl you got those guys drunk. I cannot turn my back on you for one second." said Sandra.

"I would not call it drunk, he said, just a little buzzed, I only gave them one Coors each; I knew you would be pissed if I got them drunk and I try to avoid pissing you off Sandra."

"I appreciate that Carl. She said still shaking her head. Sometimes I think there is hope for you Carl."

"I wouldn't go that far Sandra; I have had all the time in the world to become hopeless." said Carl flashing that big grin of his.

By now all five of the Indians were dancing and singing, laughing like little kids, "Jumping Jack Flash it's a gas, gas, gas!" Poe was running around with the dancing natives, he looked to be having as much fun as they were.

Carl, Sandra and I could not help but laugh watching these people dancing around singing a Rolling Stone's song.

"Good thing I didn't teach them Street fighting Man." said Carl still laughing. "Carl you are hopeless." said Sandra.

"Hey Sandra we should think about going back to the Time Dome said Carl. Maybe we can come back again sometime Sandra, but we should be leaving now."

"Wind Song, it is time we leave, we must return to our own time and space." said Sandra.

"We had so much fun today, meeting you all was such a good thing." said Wind Song. She walked up to Sandra and took her hands.

"I am so glad we met you strange people today she said. We saw much, we learned much. Riding on the big water was a great joy; I thank you for that, my friend Sandra. This was a day of much happiness I will never forget."

We had traveled back at level 3; I thought to myself, they will not remember any of this. We will seem like a dream to them tomorrow. It has to be that way with Time Traveling.

Wind Song gave Sandra a shell necklace; "Please keep this my friend Sandra with hair like the sun." Sandra reached into the cooler and told Wind Song to hold her hands together and filled them with M&Ms, "these are for you and your friends to share."

Sandra hugged Wind Song. "Will you ever return Sandra?"

Carl spoke up, "it is nice to have friends; we will try to return and find our friends again. Gray Wolf, Standing Bear, Running Fox, Smiling Water and you Wind Song, all made us happy, he said. We must go now."

I loaded the boards, the lawn chairs and picnic cooler in the truck bed. The endless cooler was just sitting there already. Damn how does that cooler do that? I had to ask myself again.

I got into the truck; Poe jumped in and sat on my lap with his head out the window. We waved at our new friends.

"Good bye said Sandra, leaning across Carl with her head out the window, I hope to see you all again."

They all waved, while singing, Jumping Jack Flash it's a gas, gas, gas, and munching on M&Ms. "Goodbye my friends." said Wind Song.

Carl took out his Zippo clicked it six times; we heard the wind sound and were back in the Dome's garage.

"Wow they are the nicest, most unspoiled people I have ever met; they are a wonder to be around." said Sandra looking at her new necklace.

"Sandra, I hate to be the one who breaks the bad news to ya, but by the year 1800 their whole tribe will be extinct. Carl was looking her right in the eyes. Everything they owned was made of wood or from animals. There is no example of their language, they found a few broken pieces of clay pots and stone arrow heads where they think their village was. There is almost nothing left of the tribe called the Cape Fear Indians. Vanished without a trace. Wiped out by disease and war."

"My God said Sandra; they are such wonderful people, what a loss. Wind Song was such a sweet person, why Carl?"

"Because they were in the way of civilization, Sandra, no reason was needed. That necklace Wind Song gave you may be the only evidence they ever existed."

As we got out of the truck we could hear the Rolling Stones playing "Time is on my side."

"I guess Time is not always on your side, I said, just ask the Cape Fear Indians."

Dumber than Mud on a Rock
Chapter 8

"Damn, that is so depressing about the Cape Fear Indians. I really like those people; they were so much fun to be around, I could not help but like them. My God the whole tribe wiped out without a trace. It's just not fair Carl." Sandra said in a shaky low voice.

"Sandra, I have found over the years that the word fair almost never enters into things, that's just the way of it. Depressing is a good choice of words Sandra, but you can't let it get to you, there will be a lot more episodes like the Cape Fear Indians to come. You are right it is not fair." Carl added shaking his head.

"Carl I am going to jump in the pool and wash the year 1414 off my body and some of the depression out of my soul. What do you say let's go for a swim you guys? I need to get wet and clear my mind she said. Come on Poe you want to go for a swim?"

That damn dog started jumping around, I have no idea if he knew what the hell Sandra was saying or he was just excited by the tone of her voice. Sandra started running toward the pool, with Poe on her heels, she dove into the deep end and that damn dog followed her in without any hesitation. "Carl, that dog is just like Sandra, part fish."

Carl and I walked over to the edge of the pool, and sat with our legs in the warm water. "Dude it is a bummer about the Cape Fear Indians, Sandra is right you couldn't help but like them, they were really nice people."

"Brian, you got to remember you are just passing through time. These things will happen, one way or another they will happen. By traveling in time you will be made aware of them. That, my friend, is the only difference. Now you know what happens and when and how, welcome to time travel Brian." Carl said in a very matter of fact way.

We sat watching Sandra and Poe playing in the shallow end of the pool without saying anything for a few minutes. Of course the endless cooler was sitting right by Carl. How the hell does it do that? Carl opened two Coors and handed me one.

It was nice sitting there in the warm North Carolina sun; in the back ground I could hear the Stones recording "talking about you, yea nobody but you. I'm just trying to get a message through."

"Hey Carl, earlier today you said you would bring me up to speed on Global Warming. Twice in the last few days you brought up the topic of Global warming and never went into any detail. First time you were talking about the natives of Bikini Island and how the island they were relocated to, Kili Island was flooded with salt water by the year 2011. The second time was today at the beach when I said it was so much wider than it is in 1974. You also said I would get a kick out of it, and then you said it was too depressing to talk about. How so dude?"

"Giddy up down the road to extinction, said Carl; global warming is the saddest laugh on the human race ever."

"Brian pollution is the major source of global warming. In 1974 it is just starting to be made public. By the year Sandra was living in 2016 it can no longer be swept under the rug by the powers that be. The signs of temperature change are way too evident to be ignored any longer. The Coast lines are washing away at an unbelievable rate, cities throughout the world are in danger of being swallowed up by the seas. Both the North and South Poles are melting at an alarming rate. Beaches all over the world are washing away. Hell they are not even washing away; they are being covered by rising water levels."

"Dude, there are major droughts all over the world. The 2016 California Sandra has been living in has been in a severe drought for years and they grow lots of food in California. Dude, it takes a bunch of water to grow the food humans eat. No water, and there is no food."

Carl's story went on.

"At the same time there is flooding in places in the world that have never flooded before. I told you Brian you would get a kick out of this."

"Large wild fires are burning down the western states, due to the lack of rain. 1000's of acres of land burned black. These fires are burning out of fucking control and taking everything in their paths. There are more fires every year and not only in the States but in Europe too." He took a deep breath and went on.

"At the same time parts of the United States are being flooded at an alarming rate, washing away towns and flooding cities. In 2017 the fucking city of Houston will be underwater because of a hurricane named Harvey. Dude, 55 or 60 inches of rain is a lot of water to be dumped on you in a few days."

"Brian this is happening all over the world, Europe is getting hotter every year and is starting to burn, big fricking forest fires there too. People are dying from the heat and it will get hotter every year and the death rate will climb." At the same time parts of that continent are being flooded. Crap, a large part of the city of Paris is under water in the spring of 2018." He continued.

"The whole world is changing and changing very fast. It is a stone cold fact if the environment changes too fast things die. Plants, animals, fish cannot adapt to the rapid climate changes; and our old buddy Mr. Extinction has a big smile on his face."

Carl just shook his head and went on with the story.

"The industrial revolution in the late 1700's is when it started to get cranked up. People moved from the country into cities for good paying factory jobs. The factories produced goods for people to spend their new found money on. That was the beginning," he said.

"The world backed itself into a corner; fossil fuels became the economic back bone of the world. Humans heat with fossil fuel, cool with it, light the dark with it, it powers almost all transportation."

"Brian, think about this, the world pumps millions of tons of Carbon monoxide into the air daily, just driving their cars to their jobs. The automobile has become a necessary evil, it created millions of jobs. Modern life is based on the automobile. At the same time automobiles are pumping poisons into the air, water and the land by the hour."

"Since the 1800's till recently a good deal of the world heated homes with coal, it was cheap, it was readily available. The cheaper the price of the coal, the dirtier it burns. Tons of coal powered factories popped up. The factories and the homes pumped billions of tons of sulfur dioxide directly into the air."

"In the mid 1800's London, England had black fog due to the burning of coal. Hell they had black poison rains, needless to say the death rates climbed. Major cities all over the world throughout the 1930's and 1940's into the 50's would be covered with black soot, due to the unregulated burning of fossil fuels."

"Still, nobody seems to care, the world is an endless garbage can, the oceans giant toilets. Factories dump untreated heavy metals directly in to rivers, lakes, streams and oceans. Rivers all over the world are still being used as toilets."

"Nobody seems concerned that humans need water to live. Dude, there is only so much fresh water in the world, there is no more. The demand goes up every day and the supplies are diminishing, due to over population, over use and pollution. At some point the day will come when people turn on the tap and no water comes out. Four or five days without water to drink and a person will die a slow lingering horrible death."

Carl spoke without looking up from the pool.

"Brian here's a really good one" he continued.

"*Plastic man made crap that never goes away.* Dude plastic is forever. I just love plastic. What a wonder plastic is, it never goes away it just sub divides itself into smaller and smaller pieces of itself and it is poison. It floats around, and sooner or later sinks. There are huge islands of plastic floating around in all the oceans of the world. By 2014 there are millions and millions of tons of the shit floating around out there. Plastic just sits there waiting for birds, fish and turtles to mistake it for food; they eat it and die a slow painful death. More or less the plastic stops their digestive systems so sooner or later whatever eats the plastic will starve, or the chemicals in the plastic will slowly poison them. Dude, they are finding plastic in fish sold in super markets, it's in the food chain. They estimate by the year 2025 over 90% of all sea birds will have plastic in their stomachs and every beach in the world will have plastic waste washed up on them."

"Later Brian we are going to take a trip and I am going to show you tons of plastic floating in the oceans, an island of floating plastic bigger then Texas, slowly poisoning the world, a thing called the Northern Pacific garbage patch. I have a few items that will scare the crap out of you that I will show you later, said a very grim looking Carl. I will lock the locations into my Zippo as soon as we finish talking. Don't let me forget."

"Okay Carl" is all I could say.

He picked up where he left off. "Dude it is cheaper to make more plastic then it is to recycle it. All the Plastic Recycled in 2016 was less than one day of the world production of the crap. By the turn of this century the world is full of plastics. You cannot look around in the year 2016 and not see plastic everywhere. Sandra's lap top, your cell phones are plastic. Buy just about anything and it is wrapped in some kind of plastic. People buy a soda, it is in a plastic bottle, they finish drinking it in a few minutes, then throw away the plastic bottle, they don't think twice about it. Nobody even notices it anymore. By the year 2025 almost everything is made of plastic or has plastic parts."

"Let's produce tons and tons of something that does not decompose Dude millions of years after all of mankind is long gone; there will still be tons and tons of plastic lying around. What a fucking joke. Make tons of something that's a poison and never goes away." Carl was shaking his head as he looked right at me.

"Brian, don't even get me started on over population. Don't forget I have been around since before the beginning of time, I remember when humans numbered in the 100's. By the year 2000 there are over 8 billion people on the face of this planet, but still people are having 4 or 5 kids or more. Excuse me but in 50 years what the fuck are these kids and their kids going to eat, each other? 8 Billion People become 12 billion People, 12 billion becomes 25 billion. Hell there is not enough food to feed everyone in the world now. Right now in 1974 people are starving to death every day" he said.

"One day the Earth will say fuck it, I can't take it anymore and there will be extinction. Dude let me tell you Mr. Extinction is a stone cold fact; I have seen him five times in the past. He is fucking real and he can be very ugly. Brian a few days ago we went back to visit the dinosaurs. It was the day before a huge comet hit the earth. Mr. Extinction hit and the dinosaurs did not have a clue. Hell we just spent this morning hanging out with a group of extinct Native Americans."

"Yesterday Brian we watched man made extinction let loose in the form of Atomic bomb tests. That fucking radiation is still out there and will be for years to come. More manmade poison."

"Every day humans pump tons and tons of poison into the air, the land and the water. Humans have done so for years and it looks like they will do so for years to come".

He looked up at me, 'What part of dumber than mud on a rock don't humans understand?"

"Brian I told you, you would get a kick out of Global warming." He kind of chuckled a little.

All I could do was stare at Carl's shining blue eyes, and shake my head. "Dude I said, so there is no hope for mankind?"

"What do you think Brian?"

I could hear the Rolling Stones recording the song "Last Time." in the back ground.

"This could be the last time, this could be the last time, maybe the last time, I don't know."

I got shivers down my spine.

Death before Disco!
Chapter 9

Sandra and Poe had gotten out of the pool and came walking up to Carl and myself. "My God Brian what happened to you, she said. I have never seen you look like this, what's wrong babe?"

I heard her but all I could do was stare at the water. I slowly looked at her and responded, "Sandra I just got slapped in the face with an over dose of reality. I was dragged into the future and it was ugly."

"I brought him up to speed on Global warming", said Carl.

Sandra sat down on the edge of the pool next to me and put her arm over my shoulder. "Damn. I keep forgetting Brian you are 40 plus years behind the world I live in said Sandra. Hell Brian, you are still more or less a hippy surf bum. Yeah the future is pretty grim Sandra said. I live in it and have got used to all that crap, ugly is a very good word to describe it Brian."

"If you think Global warming is bad wait till *Disco* hits." said Carl. Both Carl and Sandra started to laugh.

"Man if disco is as depressing as global warming I don't want to hear about it." I exclaimed.

"Brian global warming is a walk on the beach compared to disco." said Sandra. Carl and she were both almost in tears they were laughing so hard. Carl slapped me on the back and said, "Brian we are goofing on ya. You heard in a few minutes what Sandra and I have lived with for years, we are trying to cheer you up dude."

"Guys, I said global warming is one scary subject; it sounds like the way the human races does itself in, what the hell could be worse than that?"

"*Disco.*" said Sandra and Carl, at the same time, both still chuckling. "I was not born yet but I heard stories about disco and it was not pretty." She said still laughing like a fool.

They both started singing *"Woo, woo Stayin Alive, Stayin Alive."* Swaying back and forth pointing their finger in the air "Stayin alive, stayin alive, woo, woo!" They looked so fucking silly.

"Sandra, you want to take Brian to a real live Discotheque? We can Time Travel to Studio 54 in New York City in the year 1977 and take him to the top of the disco heap."

"I've been to Studio 54 more than a few times. I am on the "A" list and get right in every time I go. Good evening Carl the first. Welcome to Studio 54 come right in. They think I'm royalty."

"I must admit of all the things I have seen and done in time travel, that place was by far one of the strangest. Lots of Debauching to a boogie beat. The electronic synthesized phenomenon fueled by Cocaine and Quaaludes called Disco, promiscuity in platform shoes."

"There is always a ton of hot, well dressed beautiful women looking to play. I have had a great deal of fun debauching in that establishment, all under the flashing lights and the glow of the disco ball to an endless pounding beat of amplified syncopated electric music. Studio 54 reminds me of a Roman orgy, with a loud sound track. I rather enjoy Roman orgies. Said Carl with a big grin. Disco is a cliché in time, thank goodness it dies young."

"Do you think Brian is ready for Studio 54 Carl? K.C. and the Sunshine band and the Village People maybe more than he can handle. I can't see Brian putting on his Boogie shoes and doing the "Hustle," said Sandra.

They were both standing up by now and dancing, and singing, Stayin Alive, Stayin Alive, pointing into the air and going Woo, Woo, even Poe was dancing around.

I am not sure what a disco is but it certainly has a strange effect on these two, even the dog is getting weird.

"You are right Sandra let's start slow, said Carl. We can take him to see "Saturday Night Fever." Sandra face the fact, disco is on the way, nothing can be done to stop its coming. We can prepare Brian for the inevitable with small doses of disco at a time."

"You know Carl, disco could be a shock to his nervous system, he could suffer serious brain damage, more brain damage then he already has." she said laughing.

"Guys I said, Disco can cause brain damage? What the fuck is Disco? What the hell is a Saturday Night Fever? I asked. It sounds like a strange virus or a plague."

That really cracked the two of them up. "Yes Brian disco can be dangerous said Sandra. I see no way other than to drag him to see Saturday Night Fever."

"I sure wish I knew what the hell you two guys are talking about I said. Guys, Saturday Night fever sounds like a weird flu! A sickness that lasts for one night?" Once again the two of them lost it and busted out laughing.

Carl was grinning "Sandra let's zap up to 1977 and go catch Saturday Night Fever's premiere at Mann's Chinese Theater. We can Time Travel to Hollywood California December 14 th 1977. This is a big event, lots of the Hollywood Stars, it is a must be seen at gala red carpet affair. Everyone who is anyone will be there."

"I am not sure that would work either Carl, I can't see us rubbing elbows with movie stars, can you?"

"You are right Sandra, let's do this in small doses, we can zip up to 1977 and catch it in a local movie theater or better yet we can go to a drive in."

"Oh goodie, I want buttered pop corn and Ju-Ju beads!" Sandra said.

"Okay you two, you guys want to drag me up to 1977 to catch a fever and eat pop corn?"

Once again they broke into singing Stayin Alive Stayin Alive, with more "Woo, Woos!"

"Okay Brian I will explain said Carl. Disco is when the world goes nuts for awhile. In the late 70's and early 80's disco achieved popularity, and all these dance clubs will pop up all over the world. People would get all dressed up, do drugs, drink and dance to the Disco beat.

In 1977 they put out a movie called Saturday Night Fever. It is about a kid from Brooklyn who spends his free time dancing in Discotheques. That's what they will call these dance clubs. It's not a bad movie; it takes place in New York City a few years from now, lots of drama. Anyway he dances at a club named 2001 Odyssey. Check this out in the year 2017 the dance floor from the movie sold for over a million Dollars."

He went on. "The movie will explain disco better than we can, so we should just buzz up a few years and take you to the movies Brian."

"Going to see Saturday Night Fever on the big screen will be fun. I had seen it on cable TV, but never in a movie theater." said Sandra.

"Saturday Night Fever is a movie about an upcoming dance craze?" I asked.

"Yep, that's about the size of it, but there is no getting away from the fact, Disco is on its way. Brian sometimes you have to stand your ground and look the Devil in the eyes, better the devil you know." said Carl.

"Hey Sandra, let's go to the Ford Theater and catch it there. What do ya think?" Asked Carl.

"Carl are you talking about the place they shot Abe Lincoln? I'm not into watching John Wilkes Booth blow honest Abe's head off."

"Na, Sandra not the Ford Theater in Washington D.C. We can buzz up to Saturday July 29th, 2017 and catch the 40 th Anniversary Directors cut at the Ford Amphitheater on the Coney Island boardwalk in Brooklyn New York City. That Ford Theater holds 5000 people. May as well go all the way and see the uncut version in Brooklyn, where it took place."

Carl continued. "The movie they released in 1977 was PG. they cut the hell out of it. They cut out a lot of cussing, a fight scene, a topless dancer and the rape of the star's girlfriend."

"I can line up tickets on the Time Phone and off we go to Saturday Night Fever in the year 2017. We can leave as soon as we get cleaned up, beside Coney Island is always fun. We can have Nathan's hot dogs and cream sodas for dinner that would be so New York," said Carl.

"What about it Brian, are you up for a Time trip to 2017 Coney Island to catch the uncut version of Saturday Night Fever?"

They both started to sing Stayin alive, stayin alive, with lots of Woo, Woo's.

As I watched Carl and Sandra, dancing around making fools out of themselves, I realized, damn I'm going to Brooklyn to see a movie about disco dancing that has not been filmed yet. Until a few minutes ago I had never heard the term Disco. Now I'm going to the 40 th anniversary of a movie that will not be released for 3 more years. Today I went to Mars, I went surfing in North Carolina in the year 1414 and ate southern fried chicken and M&M's with Native Americans and now I'm going to the year 2017 to

Brooklyn New York to catch a flick about disco dancing, and it's not even 9:30 a.m. Dome Time yet. This is only my 7th day as a time traveler. Time travel can be so damn strange! *Why the hell not?*

"Let's get cleaned up, change our clothes and go to New York City, said Carl. With our translator rings we will be able understand the New Yorkers, hell we can even speak New Yorker." That statement cracked all three of us up.

It took no time for Sandra and me to get ourselves together. A fast shower and throw on shorts and sandals and Hawaiian shirts and meet up with Carl who had on a brand new "Tar Heels" tee shirt, and walk down to the time pole.

"You guys ready for this said Carl, I see you got on your Boogie shoes, looking at our huarache sandals. I got great seats 12 rows back, dead center; I heard the sound system in the Ford Theater is killer. Let me look up the number and off we go, there is a big parking lot a few blocks away we can land in, we are traveling at level 3 so even if we are seen zapping in we will not be remembered. Don't forget to push the button on your Time watches."

Sandra bent down, petted Poe, she told him to be a good dog, and guard the Dome of Time, and we will be back in one minute. As soon as she said guard the Dome his ears picked up and his little chest popped out, it was like he understood he was now a guard dog.

"That is one smart dog." I said.

Carl picked up the book of time, turned a few pages, and said I got it, he dialed about 15 or so numbers held his Zippo lighter next to the phone and hung up and said, "Ready boys and girls, next stop is Brooklyn New York, July, 2017."

Stayin Alive, Stayin Alive!
Chapter 10

I heard the wind sound and we are standing in a huge parking lot. It was late evening in midsummer New York City; it was hot, sticky, noisy and smelled like a city.

I saw a little girl about 5 or 6 years old standing a few cars away, she was pointing at us saying, "Mommy, mommy, look at the strange people, they came out of nowhere. Mommy, Looky!" she said in a louder voice stomping her foot and pointing! "Stop it dear leave the nice people alone." Her mom said without looking up at us.

"This is so exciting; Sandra we are surrounded by real live native New Yorkers." Carl looked right at Sandra and said; "*How!* I hope they don't scalp us; did you bring the M&M's?"

"Carl you are so hopeless," Sandra laughed.

"Yes I am hopeless Sandra but I have had all the time in the world to become hopeless."

It took no time for us to get up to the boardwalk, it was wide and full of moving people of different ages, sizes, and colors all wearing various outfits. We were in the middle of a loud hot summer evening "Down the Shore" in Brooklyn.

"We have got to walk up a few blocks to get to the amphitheater, come on." said Carl. Sandra was holding my hand; her head was turning back and forth taking it all in, she was grinning. "This is fantastic she said. It's like the whole City of New York took the night off and went to the beach."

The Atlantic Ocean was on our left, the beach was packed, I mean packed full with people. The sounds, and the music and smells changed as we walked. Man, even the languages changed.

"Hey Guys less than an hour ago Dome Time we were in that same Ocean Surfing in North Carolina 600 years in the past. I don't think we could even get down to the water through all those people." said Sandra.

She spoke right to me. "Dude we are walking down a crowded boardwalk on Coney Island on a steaming hot summer's evening in the year 2017. Damn we are going to a disco movie, Brian can you believe this; we are in New York City." All I could say was; *"Why the hell not?"*

Both Carl and Sandra started to sing really loud, "Stayin Alive, Stayin Alive," and not one person even looked at them, you got to love New Yorkers.

"Carl, what is that big red tower thing over there?" Sandra said.

"That is the Parachute Jump; it was built for the New York's World's Fair in 1939. Dudes I went to that Fair, I had a great time. We can go back to the 1939 World's Fair if you like. It will be fun. See that Ferris wheel, it was built in 1920; its 150 feet tall. I rode on it back in 1939, great view, you guys will love it. Over there is the Cyclone Roller Coaster, that is one fun ride too. A bunch of these rides are listed in the National Register of Historic Places. Let's make a point of going back to the 1939 World's Fair," said Carl.

"That sounds like fun, I have never been to a World's Fair said Sandra. Hell till a few minutes ago I had never been to New York City, hanging out with you Carl is always interesting to say the least. She leaned over and kissed his cheek, you are way too much fun, Carl The first."

I think I saw Carl blush. They looked at each other and both started to sing "Stayin Alive" again.

All I could do was laugh and shake my head. I live with two crazy people and we Travel in Time. *Why the hell not?*

"Coney Island is a mix of very old structures and the very new, lots of new construction, said Carl. That freak Hurricane Sandy hit this coast line hard a few years ago, back in 2011. The tidal surge was between 12 to 14 feet high. A lot of rebuilding going on since. A storm that big in late October, this far north is an example of the climate change. Sandy was totally an unreal storm. She caused 125 Billion Dollars worth of damage to the upper east coast."

"What else would you expect from a storm named after Me." said Sandra. "Named after you Sandra?" Carl and I said at the same time, looking right at her.

"But of course." she said with a flick of her long blonde hair. *Why the hell not?* I thought to myself, I could see Sandra having a Hurricane named after her.

"Hey guys said Carl by the year 2125 most of Coney Island will be underwater, our friend Global warming doing its thing. A good deal of low lying coast line throughout the world will be in the ocean within the next 100 years. On the bright side the surfing in Philadelphia will be great. Hell a huge chunk of Antarctica broke off a few weeks ago and is now floating around. It is the dead of winter down there; icebergs should not be breaking off this time of the year."

"Carl you can come up with some cheery subjects. Coney Island underwater, shaking her head. Gone forever, my God that's almost as sad as the demise of the Cape Fear Indians."

She was wearing the shell necklace Wind Song had given her as a gift; she reached up, placed her hand on the necklace and sighed.

"Come on boys and girls said Carl, Ford Amphitheater is just up the way on west 21st. Street. You guys know this show is 4 hours long; it is just not the movie. There will be a bunch of live disco bands performing their hit songs. Big name bands like the Tramps playing "Disco Inferno." We are going to hear classic disco songs like "More Than a Woman", "Rock Your Baby", "If I can't Have you." Think of it guys, live disco music dudes, this will be a trip." said Carl.

Sandra looked at me, shrugged her shoulders. "Lucky us she said, live disco bands from the 70's. A bunch of old people in platform shoes playing songs nobody has heard in 40 years. I would not miss this for the world." Said Sandra, with a laugh. I loved the sound of her laugh.

As we got nearer to Fords Theater, we started to notice people in disco outfits. "My God said Sandra; look at that guy." Some way overweight man in his late 60's with a comb over hairdo, wearing a white suit and platform shoes with his belly hanging over his belt was walking right in front of us.

"O my God that guy is way too fat to disco said Sandra, this is getting damn scary! It's like everyone raided the Goodwill for vintage clothes.

Guys we are way underdressed for this, Hawaiian shirts and sandals are so undisco."

The closer we got to Ford Theater the more crowded it got and the more disco outfits there were to be seen. All the people seemed pretty excited about this whole disco thing.

The front of the Ford Theater looks like it's from the turn of the 19th Century, the open air theater in the back was new and clean, and it was huge. The place looked like it was built to amplify sound.

We waited a little while in line to get in, thank goodness there was a bar as soon as we got inside and of course the sound system was blasting out "Stayin Alive, Stayin Alive".

"I'm beginning to hate this fucking song" I said to Carl and Sandra, who both started to dance again pointing their fingers in the air singing along with the song. All the people in the bar were doing the same thing; my God "Saturday Night Fever" has infected all of them. I had the sudden urge to run away, get a grip Brian, I said to myself you can do this, be strong. All I could do was order 3 double shots of Jameson's and shake my head. I handed Sandra and Carl their shots, a toast I said, here's to "Stayin Alive!" They both said" Stayin Alive!" and slammed back their shots.

"Wow this is a beautiful place said Sandra, so roomy."

"Come on guys our seats are way up front follow me." said Carl.

We had great seats 12 rows back in the center, we didn't have long to wait for the show to start. The host was some guy name Joe, with a real heavy New York accent, I was glad I had on my translator ring. Joe started introducing, people and acts, the music started; every song had a pounding beat. The crowd loved it, they are up and dancing in the aisles, singing along with every song, lots of "Woo-Woos."

I knew immediately I was never going to be a fan of disco. Man I am listening live to 40 year old songs that have not been recorded yet.

I must admit the movie was not bad at all, great dancing, pretty cool story; I could see why it is going to be such a popular flick.

There is no doubt that this was 4 of the longest hours of my life. The beat of each song seemed the same as the last one. The beat was working its way into my brain, Boom, Boom, and Boom! Don't get me wrong the whole show was entertaining to watch, but I really wanted no part of disco in my future. By the time the show ended I had been properly introduced to the world of disco and my head was pounding. The crowd was up and clapping and yelling and going wild. Eventually the people started moving out. When Carl asked me, "So Brian what do you think about disco?"

"What a dumb ass question that is Carl, I answered with a big grin on my face. Next time just tie me to a pole and burn me alive it would be a lot less painful than 4 hours of disco, never do anything like that to me again Carl." I laughed.

"Okay Brian. Hey dude are you sure you don't want to pick up a Saturday Night Fever poster for your room?" Inquired Carl with a twinkle in his eyes.

"I want a poster said Sandra, I thought John Travolta was cute, and I can hang it next to my Van Gogh painting." Carl and I both looked at her after that statement.

"Next to your Van Gogh,? I asked. You are going to hang a Saturday Night Fever Disco poster next to a portrait Vincent Van Gogh painted of you Sandra?" She just smiled at me. "I think John Travolta has a cute butt."

No matter what I said it would be wrong, so I said nothing and smiled back at her.

"Look guys, said Carl, we can zap out anytime we are traveling at level 3, but let's walk up to Nathan's Hot Dogs, get some hot dogs to go and have lunch while orbiting the earth in the Time shield."

"Eating hot dogs while orbiting the earth, sounds like a ton of fun. 'Sandra exclaimed.

"Yeah maybe it will get that damn disco beat out of my head." I added.

"There is a bar on the way, so we can wash away some of the disco fever." said Carl with that big Cheshire cat grin of his.

The walk to Nathan's was enjoyable, it was night and it had cooled off a lot, a nice sea breeze was blowing, the boardwalk was not nearly as full of people as it was earlier.

Carl was right; there was a great bar on the way. A double shot of Jameson's worked wonders on that Saturday Night Fever. I am so glad the Dorian effect will not let you get drunk, you get a nice buzz but are always in control, you got to love that Dorian effect.

We took our time walking to Nathans; Carl ordered 9 hot dogs with chili and onions to go. We walked down to a dark part of the beach. Carl took out his Zippo clicked it 6 times, there was the wind sound again and just like that we were standing in the North Carolina sunshine. I could hear the Rolling

Stones recording in the background, "I see my Red door and I want it painted Black, no colors anymore I want them painted Black."

Thank God for the Rolling Stones, I could feel the disco beat being pushed out of my head. I had survived my first encounter with Disco. "Stayin Alive," I said to myself.

Hot Dogs in Space!
Chapter 11

"Well guys, that was a great trip exclaimed Carl, lots of drama, I love drama. We survived Saturday Night Fever. I'm getting hungry, let's take a trip into space and pig out on Nathan's hot dogs, drink Coors, smoke hash and blast out a bunch of Rolling Stones music. We will float around space in the time shield and clear our heads. Wait till you guys see this, it is a *breathtaking* view of the earth."

As soon as Poe heard our voices he was running up towards Sandra, tail wagging, letting out a bunch of soft barks, like he was talking to her. She knelt down to pet him, saying what a good dog you are Poe. He damn near knocked her over when he leaped up and put his paws on her shoulders, he was standing there licking her face.

"That damn dog loves Sandra, she has a big heart and Poe knows it, grinned Carl. Sandra has always amazed me."

"It's time Poe took a trip in the Time Shield; he is going with us into space today. Let's blast off for lunch in space. I'm hungry," said Carl.

"Carl, I know you are starving, so am I but I would love to go for a fast swim and wash 2017 New York off me and change my clothes. Come on Carl it will not take long and we do have all of Time to play with," said Sandra. "Damn woman you know I can't say no to you, sure a fast swim and a change of clothes will work. Just keep Poe dry, he is going with us this trip."

The warm pool felt great, it helped wash some of the disco off, a fast rinse in the outdoor shower, a quick change of clothes, and we were ready for lunch in space.

I opened my closet and picked out 3 Hawaiian shirts, I put one on and walked out gave one to Sandra and one to Carl. "We cannot go eat hot dogs in space without the Aloha spirit." The shirts looked good on them.

"Hawaii Five - 0" in space I said laughing. Jack Lord would be proud of us, Book em Dano!" That cracked Carl and Sandra up.

"I warmed up the hot dogs in the oven and stuck them in the picnic cooler; the endless Coors cooler will be where it should be, next to my lawn chair, let me look up the number and off we go." Carl said, with a sparkle in his eyes.

We headed down to the time pole. "Come on Poe we are going to take a trip in space and have lunch, I brought some doggie treats for you so you won't feel left out Poe. I don't think chili dogs would be too good for you Poe." I swear that dog understands what Sandra is saying, his tail was wagging a zillion miles an hour, and he was hopping around. "Good boy Poe, you are going to orbit the earth right now, won't that be fun?" She asked Poe.

She went on. "You know guys I have spent half my life with wet hair; I hope I don't catch a cold going in to orbit with damp hair," she said. With hair as long and as thick as hers and as much time as she spends surfing I can see why she always has wet hair.

"Guys I was just thinking we can float around real close to the International Space Station and freak the hell out of the Astronauts. I can turn the Time Shields tinting to completely transparent so we can be seen from the outside. The Time Shield would be invisible to them. We would look like we were just sitting on lawn chairs, floating around in space having a picnic. I can hear it now; Astronauts report they saw aliens, floating outside the Space Station's window, sitting on lawn chairs, wearing Hawaiian shirts with a little black dog eating hot dogs, and drinking Coors. Like that won't blow some minds. We can hang out and let them take a bunch of photos. It will be fun," said Carl.

"I can bring my "Go Tar Heels" bumper sticker and hold it up for them to see. I can see The New York Times headlines. Space Aliens are Tar Heel fans!"

He chuckled. Carl was on a roll. "Check this out; Astronauts in the I.S.S. report seeing a black dog, a beautiful blonde and two Hippie looking dudes, wearing Hawaiian shirts floating 250 miles above earth, eating Nathan's hot dogs."

"Reports state they were drinking Coors and blasting out Rolling Stones music. Now that would send shock waves all over the world. I love starting U.F.O. stories," said a grinning Carl.

"Carl, how the hell do you come up with this crap?" I asked. "Brian I have had all the time in the world to become a prankster."

Why the hell not? I thought to myself.

"Hey Carl you remember the movie "The Day the Earth Stood Still" starring Michael Rennie and his robot buddy Gort? Maybe we can do something along those lines; you know deliver the people of earth a message, a wakeup call to the whole world about Global warming and plastics. What do you think?" I asked him.

"I love that movie Brian; Gort, Klaatu Barada Nikto, I memorized that line. In my line of work I never know when I might run into a giant robot and need to use it." Once again all I could do was look at Carl and shake my head.

"Yeah Carl maybe we can send a warning to the people of earth. People of Earth Stop Fucking up your planet! Be responsible with plastic, stop using fossil fuel, and get rid of nuclear weapons."

"Great idea Brian but unless we can do something to get the whole world's attention nothing will change. We have to be able to shock them into reality; we have to think about this," he said.

"Carl, the more I learn about Global warming the more pissed off I get. I want to grab everyone in the whole fucking world and shake them to their senses. Dudes wake the fuck up, your world is dying and you guys are killing it." I added strongly.

"I like Brian's idea, said Sandra. I'm sure the 3 of us can come up with some way to shock the world to its senses. Maybe float outside the Space Station with a big sign."

"YOUR PLANET IS DYING."

"Nice touch Sandra, it may work. Perhaps you guys are on to something. Let's think about it, but right now we are going to go float around in space and eat lunch, I'm starving." said Carl.

Carl picked up the gray notebook, thumbed through it, turned a few pages, dialed a few numbers on the old phone held his Zippo next to the phone, and hung up.

"I got it. We will be 250 mile high, moving at 5 miles a minute, close enough to see the International Space Station. With the shield's tint on they will not be able to see us. We can't miss the Space Station it is longer than a football field, 356 feet long and 240 feet wide." He started to dial the phone, held his Zippo next to it and hung up.

"Okay, boys and girl here we go next stop May 17th, 2017, that is the day the Space Station reported a U.F.O. sighting. I was thinking that U.F.O. they saw may have been us. Sit down guys, Sandra hang on to Poe and off we go."

Carl clicked his Zippo Twice, I heard the wind sound, it got dark really fast, and we were on our way to orbit the earth and eat chili dogs. *Why the hell not?*

"What a rush said Sandra, I love this. She reached over and held my hand, and said Brian we are going into space to have lunch." Poe was sitting at her feet, looking like he had been zapping around in time and space all his life. He was totally relaxed; he was even scratching his ear with his back foot. It took no time at all for us to zap up to 250 miles high on May 17th, 2017; we were in sight of the Space Station.

Carl was right; it was pretty damn big and looked so out of place against the back ground of the earth and stars. It was like a silver "Tinker Toy" floating above the slowly turning earth.

The earth was right under us; it looked a hell of a lot bigger than it did when we were on the moon. How many nights have I been on watch and stood on the bridge wing of a ship and stared up at these stars? Those very stars surrounded me now and looked close enough to touch.

"Let's eat" said Carl, he opened the picnic cooler and handed Sandra and I a Nathan's hot dog each and a handful of paper napkins.

He opened 3 cans of Coors, gave us both one stood up and said "A toast guys, Hot Dogs in Space."

Sandra and I stood up; we all touched our Coors together and said, "Hot Dogs in Space."

"This calls for some Rolling Stones you cannot eat hot dogs in space and not listen to the Stones it's a rule," he said with that damn Cheshire cat grin.

He reached over, plugged in the tape and "Under assistant, west coast promotion man" started to play. This will blast the disco out of our heads."

The hot dogs tasted fantastic, the Coors was ice cold, the view was *"breath taking"* and the Stones rocked on.

Plastic Fantastic Lover!
Chapter 12

We floated 250 miles above the earth munching on Nathan's hot dogs and drinking ice cold Coors. Sandra had taught Poe the dog to sit and give her his paw for his doggie treats. He seemed to pay no attention at all to the fact he was floating in a big bubble miles above the earth. He did bark when he first saw the Space Station, we told him was a good dog. He looked proud of himself, with his tail wagging. Look at me I'm a guard dog.

"That is one smart dog," I said. "Yeah said Carl, Poe is a sharp little guy. I'm glad we went back for him Sandra." "I love that little critter, thanks Carl. Saving him was a nice thing to do."

"He is your dog Sandra, no doubt about that said Carl, if he makes you happy, it makes me happy".

Carl and I had polished off 3 Nathan's hot dogs each; Sandra managed to eat one and a half. "Damn these are great hot dogs" I said. "Check this out, said Carl did you guys know Nathan's has a hot dog eating contest every summer and has for years. In the summer of 2017 one guy ate 72 hot Dogs in a ridiculously short period of time."

"72 hot dogs,? I could not even eat two of them, said Sandra. What a shame Coney Island is going to be washed away by global warming. I had fun there. It's a one of a kind place. Are we still going back to the 1939 World Fair Carl?"

"But of course Sandra, he said. It will be a gas."

"Carl is that a Jumping Jack Flash it's a gas, gas, gas?" asked Sandra, laughing out loud.

"I would not have it any other way." he said.

"Can you guys believe that we are floating in space in sight of the International Space Station? We still have 35 minutes left in this trip." said Carl. He reached over and took out the Rolling Stones tape and plugged in The Jefferson Airplane. "Surrealistic Pillow" started to play. "Man I love this record turn it up Carl, this is some great music." I said.

The song "White Rabbit" started to play. "One pill makes you larger and one pill makes you small and the ones Mother gives you don't do anything at all. Go ask Alice when she is 10 feet tall."

"It is definitely time for a bowl of Hash." I announced.

"Way ahead of you Brian," as he handed me a lit pipe, I took a big hit and passed it to Sandra. In no time the Time Shield was full of smoke. I think Poe got a bit of a buzz, he stuck his head on Sandra's lap, and she sat there scratching his head.

"Carl, have you put any thought into how we can make some kind of a worldwide wake up call. Can we even do something like that? Shock the world into opening its eyes to what is going on around them." I asked.

"Brian I have been thinking about how to go about doing something along those very lines, we have to be careful. We can't come off as some kind of divine power; we never want to cross the God line. Space Aliens speaking to earth maybe our best bet. Carl went on, I think we can use our Time Traveling power to enlighten the people of earth but we have to be careful. Shaking up the world I think we can do, but we should do it in small doses, and over a bit of time. Let them think it was their idea."

"Look below us guys said Sandra, that's the North Carolina coast, there is the outer bank. Looky is that the Cape Fear River? Man we were just surfing right down there 600 years ago and less than an hour ago dome time. Hell the Time Dome is under us right now. Time traveling loves to fuck with your head."

"You just noticed that Sandra?" Carl asked.

"Hey you two, I really liked surfing a lot, I can't wait to Cowabunga again." Sandra and I looked at Carl and shook our heads.

"We can go surfing tomorrow Carl, we can surf everyday from now on," said Sandra.

Just then the song "Plastic Fantastic Lover" started to play. "Great timing I said, Maybe we can start out by dumping a load of plastic 2 feet from the Space Station window. I mean a huge pile of plastic. We can go to the beach early in the morning on the 5th of July, with about a half dozen trash bags, and fill them up with all the plastic crap that is left behind on the sand and dump it right next to the Space Station. Floating right fucking there in their face. Nobody could ignore that. Talking about a slap in the world's face, no explanation for its existence, it was not there then it is. Plastic garbage floating in space. That would make headlines worldwide."

"Brian I'm not sure that's a real good idea said Sandra, I hate to spread pollution into space."

"Carl spoke up, you got to be kidding me Sandra, do have any idea how much manmade crap there is floating around in Space right now? Dude there is tons of manmade stuff floating around up here. There are abandoned satellites, parts of launch vehicles, debris from damaged space crafts, not to mention all the fricking satellites that are still functioning. There are satellites running into each other making more junk, some of this crap is as small as a marble; some are the size of a truck. Some of these objects are moving at 17,000 mph. Man, NASA calls it space junk. If something as small as a marble moving at 17,000 mph hits the space station it could spell disaster. They say there is about 20,000 plus pieces of manmade crap flying around up here. Adding a few plastic bottles and bags is nothing."

"Never the less we should put some real careful thought into this before we move forward with our wake up call to the world, said Carl. Right now we should just sit and enjoy orbiting the earth."

"My God, man is fucking up space too?" Sandra asked.

"Humans have a knack for fucking up everything they touch, said Carl, that's the way of it. We should carefully consider how we can make a change; we do have Time to play with."

We said nothing, for a few minutes. We floated above the earth, smoking hash, drinking Coors and enjoying the Jefferson Airplane. The view was *"breath taking!"*

My God this is only my 7th day as a time traveler. I had gone to Mars and left a Dr. Pepper bottle. I went to the year 1414 to go surfing in North Carolina and hung out with the Cape Fear Indians. I zapped up to a disco show in 2017 Coney Island New York and I just ate hot dogs in space. I am floating 250 miles above the earth, within a half mile of the International Space Station; and it's not even 9:30 a.m. Dome Time. Man, I have 500 more years of this to come. *Why the hell not?*

"Do you guys feel like fucking with the people in the Space Station? That's a good place to start our wake up call. Said Carl. We can move the Time Shield to within a few feet, then turn off the tinting so they can see us for a few seconds. We can be sitting there waving at them then disappear. Poof gone again. They reported a U.F.O. sighting on this date; I hate to disappoint them." By now Carl was cracking up laughing.

"Carl do you think we should let the people in the space station see us?"She asked.

"Sandra it's a fact they reported a U.F.O. on this date. The story goes they started filming the U.F.O and it disappeared. For all we know it was us they saw. We can turn the shields tint down to become visible and disappear just like that, nothing to it. Come on it will be fun."

"Okay Carl, but let me brush my hair first. If I am going to be a UFO I want to be a good looking UFO I wish I had some lip stick, maybe some eye liner."

"Sandra you don't wear makeup, what's up with that?" I asked. "Brian if there is a chance I will end up on the front page of every news paper in the world, I want to look my best."

"My God woman you are a stone cold knock out, you could end up being the first Space Alien on the cover of "Vogue Magazine.""

"Na said Carl, in that Hawaiian shirt, long blond hair and dark tan; I can see her on the cover of "Surfer Magazine",

"Do Space Chicks Surf?"

"Ah, cut it out you guys Sandra laughed, I am going to brush my hair. Wow, I forgot I have some lip stick in my bag. Let me freshen up some first. So what is the plan, Carl?"

"I was thinking we can move up to about 5 or 10 yards from the observation windows, sit there Invisible with the tint up, wait till we are sure there are astronauts looking out. Then POOF we turn the tint off and the music way up. We can be waving like Buddy Ebsen at the end of the TV show; the Beverly Hillbillies. 'Ya'll come back now, hear?' Wave like crazy for about 10 seconds, than Poof we are gone."

"I like everything except the waving part; I think we should look mysterious and dignified." said Sandra.

"Hey, Sandra, Buddy has an outstanding wave, he even points and he tips his hat and never misses a beat. What a fantastic waver he is. I can watch the end of that program over and over, that is an all time classic wave." Insisted Carl. "Don't get me wrong Carl, I'm not putting down Buddy's wave, I happen to like that wave a lot, a very outstanding wave, I'm just saying we should have an air of mystery about us."

"What do you think Brian, to wave or not to wave? Asked Sandra. That is the question, and you have the deciding vote."

"What do I think Sandra? I think both of you two are out of your fricking minds. The Beverly Hillbillies? You two are stone cold crazy! I live with two insane Time Travelers, we are floating 250 miles above the earth and you guys are debating Bubby Ebsen's wave. Let's get a grip boys and girls." I said shaking my head.

"Guys, I think we should put our Sun glasses on be holding a can of Coors each, and crank up Jumping Jack Flash. Let them see us giving the world the peace sign and vanish." I said.

"Brian you are still a Hippie, said Sandra. Flashing the peace sign? You are so stuck in 1967."

"Sandra, don't forget Winton Churchill's famous "V" for Victory sign said Carl."

"Winston who?" Sandra asked. "Never mind Sandra," we both said.

"Sure thing. I am up for a peace sign, it is very non offensive, okay with you Sandra?" Carl asked.

"Okay, said Sandra, peace sign it is, but we still have to be mysterious. No sticking your tongue out or picking your nose Carl, and definitely no mooning the space station you hear me Carl?"

"Ah shucks, Sandra you take all the fun out of things. Okay guys let's do this. We still have about 32 minutes left before the Time Shield zaps us back to the Dome of time." Carl started slowly moving the Time Shield toward the International Space Satiation. I could make out the Observation windows very well. The light from inside the I.S.S. came through the windows, a beam of brightness shining into the vast darkness of space.

"Man we are in luck, I said. I think I can see people in the observation tower, Yeah there is someone looking out the window. Wow it looks like a woman, oh this is going to be great."

"Wow, no fooling said Sandra, I see her too. Carl how close can you bring the Time Shield to the space station?"

"I can get us up to about 10 or 15 feet from the window said Carl. Close enough for us to look them in the eyes."

"Oh this is going to be so much fun. Okay we sit holding a can of Coors, sunglasses on, flashing the peace sign. Right? I think we should be smiling, okay with you guys?" asked Sandra.

"Yeah Sandra that sounds like a plan." Said Carl, with that stupid grin of his. "No high jinks Carl, you have got that look on your face, and you are such a juvenile Carl. How does my hair look? asked Sandra, this is so exciting." She said with a chuckle.

We could see a woman with brown hair looking right out the window at the space the Time Shield was in. What amazing luck, yelled Carl. "Here we go, we are turning visible!"

I could very clearly see the woman in the space station mouth form the words *"Oh my God."*

She turned and yelled to someone and in a few seconds a man's face appeared next to her. They turned and looked at each other and I am pretty sure "what the hell" was said.

We sat in the Time Shield 15 feet from the I.S.S. in our lawn chairs, sporting our Hawaiian shirts, sunglasses on, giving the world the peace sign.

Carl was behaving himself; Sandra flicked her hair, while petting Poe the dog, they both had huge smiles,

"Jumping Jack Flash" was blasting out.

I took a drink of cold Coors and thought *Why the hell not?* Man I love Time Travel. We sat there about 15 seconds and Carl turned the tinting back up on the Time Shield and we disappeared. We could still see the two astronauts talking in excited motions as Carl backed the Time Shield back into the endless blackness of space.

"Dude that was so cool said Sandra; did you see their faces when they saw us? "Oh my God" was the right response. One way or the other our wake up call to the world is under way. I think that was a great place to start."

"Looky guys we still have about 25 minutes before we zap back to the Dome of Time, I have a few things I want to show you first. This trip will be something you two will never forget; it will be a major wake up call. Okay with you guys?" Asked Carl.

Sandra and I looked at each other; "Carl is on a roll" she said to me.

"Sure thing Carl lets go," we both said at the same time.

Death Takes a Holiday.
Chapter 13

"This trip is going to be an eye opener for you two." said Carl. "More so then the Atomic bomb trips Carl?" Asked Sandra.

"Yep, what I am going to show you two next serves no purpose at all. The Atomic bombs tests in a weird way helped to prevent the 3rd World War. In man's bizarre way of thinking it was the lesser of two evils. A few controlled blasts to scarce the crap out of the other guy, or the distinct possibility of total nuclear war. So in its own perverted way the atomic bomb tests may have served a purpose. That is about as close as I can come to justifying the nuclear bomb tests. They were more or less a brief flash in the pan compared to Plastic. Plastic never goes away, never dude. Wait you will see for yourselves. I am going to show you guys 4 items that will make you sick.

The things you will see are gross and disgusting and worst of all are real and happening now."

"Here is my plan Carl said with a very strange look on his face, We are going to zap down to 20 miles above the earth and head out west a ways, turn north and go up the Pacific coast, and then head west again out to open ocean. Then buzz south a few 1000 miles to the most remote island in the world, then head east to the Gulf of Mexico then turn north and back to the dome. This will not take very long 15 or 20 minutes tops. When we get back to the Dome we will have much to talk about."

"This trip is going to slap you in the face, Carl said looking right at Sandra and me. First we are going to check out a bunch of forest fires. Huge portions of the western states are on fire burning out of control, destroying millions of acres of land. We will buzz by some of the hot spots, pardon my pun. Global warming is real and happening as I speak. Wait and you will see for yourselves." Carl continued with his plan.

"Then we are going to swing out to the 'Great Northern Pacific' garbage patch." 100's of thousands of tons of plastic floating around, stuck between two major currents, just sitting there floating. This patch of plastic is twice the size of Texas, millions of tons of the shit up to 9 feet deep. Breaking down into smaller pieces of plastic every second. These little bitty fragments are called microplastics. Each little tiny particle of plastic is floating poison that will never fully decompose. Just floating around waiting for some poor creature to eat it and die a slow painful death. Plastic is in the food chain and has reached the point that humans are consuming it. I will never look at fish sticks the same way." said Carl.

"If we get there at the right time of day the sun light reflecting off the floating plastic derby can be *breath taking."*

Sandra and I turned to look at each other. "Breath taking?" We said nothing, Carl is on a roll.

"After we take in the sights of this man made wonder of floating plastic garbage, we will head south and explore an uninhabited tropical island that is totally covered with plastic. A little place called Henderson Island, covered with over 17.5 tons of plastic."

"Here's the good part, this island is the most remote island in the world. Great place to bring the family. Sea shell hunting is so passé. I wonder how many disposable lighters the kids can find in an hour, lots of fun for the whole family." Carl laughed.

"Then we Zap east to the Gulf of Mexico and take in a favorite spot of mine "the Dead Zone." It is such a catchy name, the Dead Zone. You guys will love this place, so romantic, brown poison water, miles and miles and miles of it, just killing everything in its path. This patch of floating death is bigger than the state of New Jersey and is growing all the time; it has its own ambiance. Wait; you guys will see for yourselves."

"So what do you guys think; you want to get grossed out by stupidity and greed?" asked Carl.

"Carl till 7 days ago I was living in 1974, I had no idea how dire pollution and global warming would become in a short amount of time. Nobody even spoke of these things in 1974. Yeah I want to see this. The more I learn about global warming and pollution the more pissed off I get. I have got to do this Carl. Are you in Sandra?"

"Damn right I'm in Brian. You know what really pisses me off? I lived in 2016 and these major items get very little or no news coverage. There is almost nothing in the newspapers, on T.V. or the radio about this man made mess. The internet should be screaming this out, but not a fucking word. Maybe a brief passing spot on the evening news but that's it. But let some Hollywood cleavage queen starlit break up with her boy friend and the world is at her door. Wake up people, large parts of the world are on fire. There is tons of plastic floating in the oceans all over the world, and parts of the world are flooding. That should be in everyone's face every fucking day, she spoke in a soft but very firm voice. Yeah damn right I'm going, what's the plan Carl?"

"Okay, you are both in on this. I hope you guys are ready for this; it will be shocking. I looked up the locations and locked them into my Zippo before I left the dome. This will be intense guys."

"Hey Carl, I've wanted to ask you about your Zippo lighter since I first saw it. You Time travel by locking numbers into it, you click it open and closed a few times and there we are, and then you light a pipe full of hash with it. It's a cigarette lighter you programmed to time travel. Do you know how fucking strange that sounds? But knowing you better now Carl it is not that strange after all. Do you ever worry you will lose it and you will get stuck someplace in Time?"

"Brian I love this Zippo; I have had it since before the beginning of time. It has always lit on the first try, and I have never had to add lighter fluid to it, not ever. Check this out, it will light under water, I can use it as a flash light, and I can cook with it."

"Dude I cannot lose it, it always returns to me, like always dude. I can throw it as hard as I can; it will go flying about 20 feet, slow to a crawl and return to my hand. It think it's part Labrador retriever, it loves coming back to me, kind of a game it likes to play. More than once I had people try to steal it from me. As soon as they try to make off with it, the damn thing will light itself and send out a huge flame, the thieves are lucky if they don't get flambéed." Carl had a big grin on his face.

"That lighter has taken me to and from more places then I can ever hope to recall. I needed a hand held Time Travel devise. You got to remember when I programmed it was a long, long, long time ago. There were not a lot of things to work with lying around and I had plenty of time on my hands. I even named it "Bob," Yep! Bob the Time Traveling Zippo lighter."

"I only smoke Camel cigarettes to make Bob happy; he gets a big kick out of lighting cigarettes. It's in his blood; after all, deep down Bob is just a cigarette lighter."

"Bob." Only Carl the first could come up with that, naming a Time Traveling Zippo lighter Bob.

Carl looked over at Sandra and me and said "It's time to go boys and girls we have 21 minutes and 37 seconds before the shield returns back to the Time Dome. Say good bye to the space station said Carl; we will see them again in a different time."

"Hot Dogs in space was such a great idea Carl, said Sandra as she started to laugh; did you see the look on the faces of the people in the space station when they saw us? That alone was worth the trip into orbit. I could see the words 'Oh my God', coming out of the astronaut chick's mouth. You are so right Carl Time Travel is a ton of fun."

"Yeah Sandra fucking with the people in the Space station was a load of fun; I can't wait to see if they keep it a secret or not. You two get ready said Carl; the next stop is the world on fire. The next 20 minutes will be shocking; you guys will never forget what you are going to see in the next 1200 seconds."

But it's All Over Now.
Chapter 14

"Say good bye to the Space Station boys and girls Carl said, we are on our way to about 5 miles north of Los Angeles on the night of September 1st 2017, to check out the "La Tuna" wild fire burning near Burbank, that's real close to downtown LA. The La Tuna fire is not that big of a fire, it burned just over 7,000 acres. We are going to start out about 10 miles above the fire and check it out from way up there, and then we will move down to about 100 yards above the ground and get a real upfront look at the fire. We will hang out a few minutes so we will get a great look see at the flames."

Carl continued, "Then we are going to head back up, this time to 20 miles high and zoom north moving at 250 miles a minute. It will take us 4 minutes and 45 seconds to get to Seattle Washington, what a great rush Carl grinned, you guys will love it. When we get up to Seattle we will move to day light and then head out to the Great Northern Pacific garbage patch, I have an action packed 20 minutes planned for you guys. When we zip from L.A. all the way up to Seattle we will be travelling at night and 20 miles up so we can see how extensive these wild fires are burning. There are 100's of fires of various sizes burning all the way up the west coast as far as Alaska.

We will be able to see for miles and at night the fire will stand out against the dark back ground. Prepare yourself, these fires are burning in several states at once, the smoke from these fires is blowing all the way out into the Atlantic Ocean." Carl grinned as he looked at us.

"Our first stop is 10 miles above LA, September 1 2017." Then he clicked "Bob" the Zippo lighter twice.

I heard the wind sound. It was dark and quiet, above us are the flickering of stars. Below I could see the lights of L.A. stretching out for miles, all the way from the dark black of the ocean up to the mountains, the lights of homes, business, street lights blended into one blanket of light. The car headlights look like a long white snake with a red tail moving on the dark roads way below us.

The bright dancing glow of the fire was overwhelming, so much brighter then the background lights. It moved as if it had a life of its own, it would expand upward in a burst of energy and slowly lay back down again. The light of the fire lit the night sky with a bright yellow and red glow, as it raced down the slopes of the hills. Even from 10 miles above I could see the fire jump in front of itself and start a new blaze that was overtaken by the tremendous ball of flames. The area the moving flames covered was large and growing as I watched.

Poe the dog stood up and stuck his head on Sandra's lap; she petted him saying "It's Okay Poe." He stretched and lay down under her lawn chair and went back to sleep. "Thank God that dog can sleep through anything, all this is very intense," she said.

Below us the leeward side of the fire was covered by black thick smoke casting its dark shadow over the ground below. The smoke stretched from the ground and looked to be damn near as high as where we sat in the Time Shield. Even in the darkness of the almost moonless night I could see the long trail of the dark gray poison stretching eastward. Like the fire, the cloud of smoke had a life of its own, blowing with the wind, its shape constantly changing as it moved. I could not see the ground below the smoke its dark shadow had completely obscured any light.

There was no sound in the time shield, the sight of the huge swaying fire had taken the words from our mouths, and all we could do was stare at the glowing flames.

Nothing could be said to express my feelings at that moment, I felt like the fire was pushing on my chest and ripping my guts out. "This is not a fire I said in a weak voice, we are watching a living thing."

"Every living thing in the world needs to consume life in order to live itself. Fire is no different, it needs to feed itself. Yeah, in its own way fire is a life form."

Carl continued. "There are lots of strange life forms out there and they all need to eat. Later I will tell you guys about the "Death Floaters." Talk about a strange life form, best part is nobody even knows they exist but you hear about them almost every day. Don't let me forget to tell you about the Death Floaters, that story will shock the shit out of you." Carl said with a big smile.

"Brian we are sitting above a huge wild fire at night, fucking California is burning to the ground below us and Carl is talking about "Death Floaters" shocking the shit out of us. I am not sure what they are, and I'm not sure I want to know. What the hell can be more shocking than this?" Sandra asked in a very soft voice.

"More about that later, grinned Carl. Now let's zoom down to 100 yards above the flames and check it out close up for a little while. Then we will zip back up to 20 miles high and head north at 250 miles a minute. We will witness dozens of fires of various sizes all burning as we zoom north. But first let's go get a close, personal look at the fire below us."

He clicks his Zippo once and we started to descend downward at an unbelievable rate of speed. We sat in the time shield; the bright light of the fire lit up the shield, there was no shadows inside the shield, just a blinding light that surrounded us. The glowing light seemed as bright as the sun and was in constant motion. It moved and twisted; it jumped upward, and plunged down again, an unreal sickening dance of flames, some coming almost as high as the shield. We could hear the roar of the fire, the sounds made by the burning fire are deafening, cracking and pops louder than the constant roar of the out of control flames below us. Poe stood up and started a low growl; Sandra held on to him and told him everything is okay and that he was a "Good boy." He slowly lay down with his head right by her feet, he was definitely guarding his Sandra, he is one smart dog and he loved Sandra no doubt about that.

The fire was racing down the slope of the hills faster than a man can run. We could say nothing; the sight of the fire was overwhelming. We watched as the fire jumped over a two lane road and cover a small group of houses in flames, these houses did not catch fire; they just instantly became part of the fire. The fire all at once turned them into bright glowing flames, jumping 100's of feet into the sky. The houses that had been someone's home were gone, and the fire kept moving in its downhill race.

I looked at Sandra, her mouth was open, she was shaking her head, she turned and looked at me then at Carl and said "Before I moved into the time dome with you two guys, I lived not far from here; I could have seen this fire from my old place. Hell I was born in California, it was my home till 2016 and now it's on fucking fire below me."

"This is a great time for me to point out a few facts to you Sandra, 2017 California had over 9000 wild fires, the most in years, and the fires burned almost a million and a half acres of land. These fires killed 43 people and damaged or destroyed 10,000 structures and that was just the fires in California."

Carl went on. "Think about all the ash and smoke going into the atmosphere, mother fucking poison floating in the wind, It has got to come down someplace. Check this out, the smoke holds in the heat of the sun and speeds up global warming. It's a big wheel and it just keeps spinning. The warmer it gets the more fires there are, the more fires there are the warmer it gets. Carl continued. It's not just California, man there are 10 states burning as I speak. Dude check this out in 2017 there are wild fires burning in Ireland, can you believe that, they had 75 % less rain fall then normal and the Emerald Isle is catching fire."

He grinned and said "Happy St. Paddy's Day. The wheel is spinning, place your bets Ladies and Gentlemen."

Carl took one look at our faces and said "Enough of this. Let's buzz north, this ride will be a trip." He said. He clicked his Zippo twice and we were 20 miles high in the night sky and moving at 250 miles a minute.

The immediate rush of travelling at 250 miles a minute is incredible. Carl was right; at 20 miles up we could see for miles, he was also right about the vast amount of fires burning.

Sandra looked at me; she had the saddest look on her face; she held my hand and squeezed it hard. We could see dozens of fires as we zoomed north.

Some of the fires were quite small others much, much larger in volume and intensity. We went by them so fast; so many bright flames buzz by below, it was hard to comprehend all, I had to take several very deep breaths.

"This is really happening Brian, Sandra sighed, and it's happening right now, this is real, California is burning, and we are watching as it is happening."

The coast of California is more or less one long line of lights. San Francisco and Oakland buzzed by on our left in no time and we could see the lights of Sacramento way off on our right. There are spaces of darkness before the next glow of the cities and towns came into sight, all throughout were the fires. Four minutes and 45 seconds flew by and the lights of Seattle came into view and the shield came to a stop. We floated 20 miles high on the outside edge of the city of Seattle.

Below we could see lights of the city stretching out before us for miles. Poe looked around for a few seconds and went back to sleep. Sandra reached under her chair and petted him. "I love this mutt, he is such a mellow dog."

"Drat." Said Carl in a sudden loud voice, "we forgot to bring the marshmallows with us, you guys want to go back to the La Tuna fire and toast a few Marshmallows?"

"Carl you are out of your damn mind said Sandra; go back to that living hell? I never want to see anything like that again." Carl broke out laughing.

"We have three more stops to make before we get zipped back to the time dome; next stop is the Northern Pacific garbage patch."

"I hope you guys are having fun, Carl said. He still had a big grin on his face. Hang on boys and girls the next stop maybe the most disgusting thing you will ever see."

Going, Going, Gone
Chapter 15

Carl looked at his Zippo. "We are a little behind schedule, he said. Our next stop is the Great Northern Pacific garbage patch. You two will love this; thousands of tons of plastic floating in the sub tropical waters half way between Hawaii and the west coast. Stuck there between currents and winds and growing larger every day. All kinds of sludge, chemicals and buoyant crap end up out there floating till they fall apart but they never fully decompose. Some of this crap has been out there since the 1960's. The garbage patch is twice the size of Texas. I just Love Plastics. A poison that never ever goes away, it just breaks down into smaller pieces and becomes a thing called microplastics, little tiny bits of plastic that are mistaken for food by fish, birds, and turtles, etc. Dudes this is the world's largest collection of floating garbage. Don't get me wrong, there are lots of other garbage patches floating in every ocean and sea in the world, but let's start out big."

Carl clicked his Zippo twice, we heard the wind sound, it got light out in an instant and we were travelling in time to noon on September 2, 2017. We came to a stop and sat a few yards above the gentle swell of the deep pacific as it moved across the water, great globs of crap below us slowly move with the waves.

The ocean swell lifted the barnacle covered man made disgusting mess in a fluid motion; the collection of rank debris banged and bounced off each other as the waves passed under it. This floating monster of tossed away trash went on as far as I could see; it went from horizon to horizon. Most of the floating mess was plastic, all different kinds of plastic, bottles, foam cups, fishing nets and gear, kids toys, beach balls and plastic lighters, egg cartons, and just plain unrecognizable plastic crap. A massive accumulated obscene mess of disposable single use items.

I felt sick to my stomach just looking at the floating mess. Man it looked like plastic vomit, a mess of indistinguishable items, bits of this, parts of that, all covered with slime and oil and seaweed. Almost everything I could see was a onetime use and toss away item, like empty soda bottles that had turned green with slime and were covered with barnacles. Carl was right again, this is a disgusting sight and it is all manmade. I could see a number of fish floating belly up rotting in the water in and around the plastic, there were dead seabird's bodies decaying on larger floating hunks of the plastic. This floating garbage patch is killing as it sits here.

"I deliberately brought us to this location, this is one of the densest concentration of plastic in this whole floating mess, I wanted us to get the full effect." Carl informed us.

"My God, I said. This is floating greed, stupidity and laziness all rolled into one and it is killing the oceans and nobody is doing a fucking thing about it."

"Let's buzz up in altitude about 25 miles and get a good look at the vastness of this disgusting floating pile of manmade crap. Even that high up we will not be able to see the outsides limits of this floating shit. It is twice the size of the state of Texas, that's over 1500 miles wide. This crap is up to 9 feet deep in places. There are all kinds of life forms attracted to this floating hunk of hell. Out in the open ocean small fish are attracted to items floating in the water, they hide under it. Little fish attract bigger fish and so on. As the plastic falls apart into smaller microplastics, tiny pieces of plastic will look like food to the fish. They eat it and are eaten by larger fish and poof there is plastic in the food chain." Carl was shaking his head as he said this.

Check this out. "The fish, birds or turtles that eat this crap will starve to death with stomachs stuffed full of plastic or the chemicals that make up the plastic will slowly poison them."

He clicked his Zippo once and zap we were floating 25 miles above the pile of floating waste. From that high up us could see nothing but floating garbage for miles in every direction. This crap looks alive; it almost looked like it was breathing as the sea swell gently rolled under the gross pile of accumulated floating plastics. It moved up and down with the swell in a rhythmic motion.

"My God why are they not cleaning this up Carl?

Sandra asked loudly. Look how much shit is out here, miles and miles and miles of plastic crap. People have to do something about this. Man I surf in this water; I have spent hours of my life floating in this water. My God what are we doing to the world?"

Carl spoke up, "there is money to be made producing plastic but there is no profit in cleaning up the mess it makes, there is no money to be made in saving the world. If this was a pile of floating aluminum cans you would have bag people swimming out here to collect the cans, but used plastic has no value so here it sits. It is cheaper to make more than it is to collect and recycle the old plastic into new items. Sandra, most of the world is unaware this is out here, or they simply just do not care."

"Countries all over the world choose to ignore this floating garbage rather than spend any money cleaning it up. The United States alone will spend billions and billions on weapons. As far as I know not one cent is being spent on plastic clean up. The world is slowly being poisoned every day, but hey I feel so much safer knowing we have a state of the art 13 billion dollar Aircraft carrier or two or three or a dozen to protect us from the evil powers that be."

"Hey, Mr. World leaders wake the fuck up! If this mindless dumping of plastics into the oceans of the World continues, there will be nothing to protect us from because everyone in the world will be fucking dead."

"World leaders my ass, what part of extinction don't you guys understand? Dude, the money spent by all the countries around the world in one year on weapons to kill people would be enough to pay for the cleanup of this entire ocean going mess. Ah, but saving the world is not nearly as much fun as having a great big pile of brand new shiny things that kill. I mean really, how many shiny things do they really need?"

Carl had a frightening look on his face and his voice had a cold sound.

"Dude this really pisses me off, all the money spent to pay for the dozens of little wars going on right now as I speak would clean up this entire mess."

"Here is a great idea, how about everyone just stops all the wars for one whole week. Hey guys take a week off and kick back. Get nice and comfy on the couch, put your feet up and watch old "Three Stooge's" reruns, drink a few cold brews and not shoot anyone for one whole week. Just park the bombers and tanks and ships and take the week off. Yep you got it, no killing for seven days and nights that is 168 hours without fighting. Let spend all that money wasted on wars to clean up this huge man made mess."

"Ah, but that would make sense, can't have any of that, making sense may lead to World Peace then where would we be? You know what they say "Peace is Hell." And the beat goes on."

Carl was looking right at us, as he kept talking. "I just love my old buddy Mr. Extinction, he is so sneaky and he is so real and he is so good at his job and don't forget he is forever. The powers that be have done a great job of hiding all this impending doom from the public."

Carl went on. "To tell you the truth what really scares me is, even if the public was slapped in the face with the danger of plastics they will not do anything about it. Yep he said, that's what really spooks me."

"Hey, I told you guys the sun reflecting off the floating garbage would be breathtaking Carl said laughing. So what do you think guys, is this not a wonder to behold?"

"Breathtaking? A wonder to behold Carl? Exclaimed Sandra. Carl you have a way with words dude, this is a giant fucking mess floating in plain sight and yet nobody is doing anything about it. This pile of plastic shit alone is reason for us to go ahead with some kind of wake up call to the world. Wake the fuck up world the planet is dying and humans are killing it."

"Sandra, Carl said. We will talk more about a wakeup call to the world when we get back to the Time Dome. We still have 7 minutes and 22 seconds and two more stops to make before we get zapped back to the dome of time, this will be close."

"Next stop is Henderson Island the most remote island in the world and it is smothered in plastics, this will be a ton of fun. Lots of drama, I just love drama."

I still felt sick, I was totally disgusted by what I was looking at floating below me and I was now on my way to see more of the same.

"I think Sandra is right Carl we have to do something to make the world aware of this floating death."

"I do think something can be done Brian, later we will talk more." Carl stated in a very matter of fact tone.

Carl asked. "Hey you guys want a Coors?" For the first time ever Sandra and I replied at the same time "No thanks Carl."

"I think I would throw up if I drank a beer right now." Said Sandra. "Yeah the Northern Garbage Patch is pretty gross Carl agreed. It makes me sick just looking at it," he said.

"Okay boys and girls he continued here's the plan. Let's head down to Henderson Island. We are going to buzz back 400 years to September 2 1617, before the island was discovered and take a good look at an untouched Tropical island. Then while we are sitting in the same place we will zap back up to 2017 again 400 years in the future and see if we notice any changes. It's kind of like show and tell. We don't have much time left in this trip." he said looking at his Zippo.

Carl clicked the lighter twice, we heard the wind sound and we were on our way to Henderson Island in the year 1617. Thank God we were leaving the Great Garbage patch behind, man I still felt like I could puke.

We came to a stop about a mile above Henderson Island.

"I want us to get a good look at the place now in its untouched state, before we zap back up to 2017." Carl said.

I immediately felt better just looking below at the clear blue pristine water and the untouched clean white sand. The vivid colors of the reefs were so clear and bright; they helped clear my head of what I had just seen in the last 13 minutes. Those damn fires and the plastic floating mess of garbage; both had been a huge wake up call to me.

I took a deep breath. I had gone from sitting above an endless floating pile of Plastic crap to a virgin tropical island as fast as Carl can click a Zippo twice. We sat on the north side of the tiny island and I felt much better just being here. This Island is beautiful; there are steep cliffs behind the narrow white beaches, heading up about 20 or 30 yards to the green growth of the jungle, with a clear blue sky and water so clean you can see the reef 30 feet deep, man I would like to live here I said to myself. I felt so much better just sitting here enjoying this pristine untouched bit of heaven sitting below me.

"Hey Carl we got time for a bowl of hash?" I said.

"Dude there is always time for a bowl he chuckled."

"Hey Brian check out that reef break over there, it almost looks like we could surf it, Sandra pointed, my God this place is beautiful. I think I would like that Coors now, how about you Brian, up for a beer?" She asked.

"Sure thing a Coors sounds good." I said as I took a toke off the pipe and handed it to Sandra. "Yeah this place is fantastic; I have never seen anything quite like this before, it's like the Garden of Eden without any snakes." I added.

"Enjoy it, because it is going to change very fast, said Carl as he checked his Zippo. We don't have much time left, but let's enjoy this for a little while longer."

Poe had got up and was walking back in forth in front of us; he put his paw on Sandra's leg and started making soft dog noises. "I think Poe may have to visit the "little dog room." She said with a concerned look on her face.

"Please No doggie mistakes in the time shield Carl said to Sandra, we will be back in the dome very shortly. If Poe really needs to go potty we can zap back to the time dome right now, we can always come back here again anytime we want too." Sandra was holding Poe's head in her hands; she looked at Poe's little face and said to Carl,

"I think he will be okay for a little while, and you are right we can zip back to the dome if we need to, but I don't think we will have any mistakes Carl."

"Okay Sandra he is your dog." Carl took out his Zippo, clicked it twice and we came to a stop 10 feet over the same beach 400 years later in the year 2017.

Sandra almost screamed. "Look at all this crap, my God, they fucked up paradise again, it is gone, tons of plastic, and look at all those balls washed up, all kinds of different size balls everywhere,100's of them, and look at all the bottles, both glass and plastic. My God there are 100's of plastic razors, lighters, and damn tooth brushes, and tons of kid's toys. What the fuck is wrong with these people? Is everyone in the world blind?"

"Sandra I read a paper about this island, they said it was not only the most remote island in the world, it was also the most polluted. The 18 tons of plastic that is washed up on these beaches is less than thirty seconds worth of the world annual production of plastic. The world makes tons of this crap in less than thirty seconds. The research paper said there is about 700 pieces of micro plastics per square meter below us, lots of crap sitting on and just below this sand."

"You guys will love this story, Carl went on. The plastic boom started in World War II and in 1950 they produced 2 million metric tons of this crap a year. By 2014 it was almost 400 million metric tons. Check this out, 85% of plastic ends up in landfills; dude that is about 380 metric tons is being shoved into landfills. What a good idea, let's just cover the crap up and hide it. You just have got to love it." Carl grinned.

"Oh yeah, while I'm thinking about it, he said I want to remind you guys Plastic is used in making Polyester. I warned you both about Time Traveling with anything made with Polyester, never forget that polyester Kills."

"No kidding guys Polyester is a mindless, heartless killer Carl said. Polyester gets very weird when it time travels, a synthetic gone insane, it takes on an evil life of its own. Never, ever Time Travel with anything made with polyester."

"I remember when you told me polyester started the Black Death in middle Ages and wiped out half of Europe." I said to Carl.

"Polyester kills?" Sandra asked.

"I told you that years ago Sandra, never time travel with anything made with Polyester."

"Sorry, I forgot Carl."

"Not a good thing Sandra, in your time travels you may have set Polyester loose on the world without you knowing. I have to admit I messed up a few times and traveled with small items made with a Polyester blend said Carl. Remember in 79 A.D. when Mount Vesuvius blew up and buried Pompeii under tons of ash? That eruption was started by some Polyester I didn't know I had with me. No shit; Polyester is so sneaky and it is downright mean. Thank goodness Polyester only has a very short life span. I will fill you in with all the time travel rules again later Sandra, and there will be a quiz." he said cracking up.

I had to look at Carl and shake my head, I am never sure if he is putting us on or not, killer Polyester?

Why the hell not?

Carl went on with the plastic story without missing a beat. "Check this out. In the year 2011 Britain drinks sixteen million plastic bottles of water, soda etc. a day. No fooling, one year's worth of England's empty bottles placed end to end would go around the world 31 times. Dude, England is a small country. This is going on in almost every country in the world and it's going on every fucking day. If the current rate of production keeps up worldwide there will be 12 Billion metric tons of this stuff in the world by 2050 and God knows where it will all end up. I love finishing up on a cheerful note." He laughed again.

"A cheerful note asked Sandra? Carl you have such a strange sense of humor, you can laugh at some of the most disgusting things I have ever seen. You are cracking up and I am totally grossed out."

"Sandra, it's all in your point of view, always look on the bright side of things."

"Carl, I just watched the western states burning down, I was floating over miles of plastic crap and you are telling me to look on the bright side, man you are out of your mind Carl, what bright side?" she asked. "Sandra you been made aware of these monstrous things, now you can start doing something about them. That is the Bright side Sandra, one person, one good idea has changed a lot of things in history. But ya got to start someplace, we will talk when we get home." He said as he took a toke off the pipe.

Man as I was sitting there listening to Carl and Sandra talking and it just struck me, I have been Time Traveling for seven days now.

I am on my way to a place called the "Dead Zone" and it is not even 9:30 a.m. Dome Time and have 500 plus years of Time Traveling to come. Brian you are definitely going to have to make a lot of major adjustment to your old way of thinking. I said to myself. But man I really do love Time Traveling.

"We don't have much time left in this trip; Carl said and looked at his Zippo, we have 2 minutes and 20 seconds left Dudes. That's cool we need to get Poe home, he added when you got to go you got to go."

"We are going to zap over to the Gulf of Mexico and take a quick look see at the dead zone; it is such lovely shades of browns. We are on our way to 10 mile high and 30 miles off the mouth of the Mississippi River." He clicked his Zippo twice; we heard the wind sound and were on our way to the Gulf of Mexico on September 2, 2017.

The BEAT GOES ON
Chapter 16

There was no mistaking the fact we were over the "Dead Zone". There was a very well defined line in the water, on one side it was the blue green color of the living Gulf of Mexico, on the inland side heading towards the distant shore the water was a sick disgusting brown color that looked like floating liquid shit. I know that sounds gross but that description is not nearly as gross as what we were looking at 10 miles below. From that high up we could see ship traffic sailing through this God awful mess, the ships leaving a swirling mass of disgusting water in their wake kicked up by the props. Waves of brown water rolled away from the vessels in long flowing lines off their bows. The border between the two colors of water was very clearly defined, on one side is life on the other side is manmade brown death.

"I wanted us to see this thing from up here so we could get a good idea how massive it is, the Dead zone is every bit as gross as the Northern Pacific Garbage patch, maybe more so, because this brown water is almost an instant killer. Carl looked at his Zippo and said we are almost out of time. You guys had to see this. No trip to these sites of impending doom hanging over the world's head like the sword of Damocles would be complete without a trip to one of the dead zones. Yep, you heard me right, one of the dead zones. There are over 400 of these dead zones floating around in the waters of the world, hell there are even some fresh water lakes that have dead zones. Let's zap down and take a real close look."

He clicked his Zippo twice and in the blink of an eye we were floating about 20 feet over the line that divided the two colors of water. Floating on the edge of the brown water were 100's of dead fish of different sizes and types, it was like they swam into the brown poison made it in a few feet and died. They floated in a long row on the outside edge right next to brown water. The line of dead fish was only a few feet wide, running parallel to the brown water, and went on for as far as I could see. The damn brown water almost looked solid, like a wall floating in the Gulf; the edge was very well defined.

"Dudes, Carl said pointing at the long line of floating dead fish, 40% of all sea food in the U.S. comes out of this Water."

"The Gulf of Mexico is second only behind Alaska in fish production. The dead zone is forcing fishing boats to go out farther into the gulf before they can fish."

"A good deal of fish species live and breed in the wet lands and in brackish water nearer to the coast. Crabs, oysters and mussels not to forget dozens of different kinds of sea grasses, have called that water home for countless centuries and they cannot pick up and move."

"Think about that for a second, a lot of it is now oxygen deprived poison water. In less than 200 years mankind has managed to destroy millions of years of evolution."

"Mr. Extinction is forever." Carl started laughing.

"Man looking at all these floating fish makes me want to stop and pick up a few fish sandwiches on the way home." Sandra and I both sat speechless.

"Hey guys, till a few days ago I was a merchant seaman I worked on the big ships. I have sailed in the Gulf of Mexico many times. Hell I have even driven huge ships up the Mississippi River as far as New Orleans. In the early 70's I never noticed anything like this, of course the water got darker the closer I got to the mouth of the Mississippi, but it sure as hell looked nothing like this. All this has come about in the last 40 years. How the hell can this go unnoticed?" I asked looking at Carl.

Looking right back at me, he took a deep breath and said, "Brian my friend it's like this, low oxygen levels in the water cause these dead zones. Agriculture is the major contributor, huge amounts of nutrients from fertilizers, and tons of untreated livestock wastes are washed away by heavy rains, flood waters and melting snow and end up in streams, creeks, rivers, lakes and eventually into Oceans and seas and here into the Gulf. The extra nutrients promote rapid algae growth that sucks all the oxygen out of the water. Any living thing caught in these oxygen depleted areas more or less suffocates, dude what a charming way to die."

"The mighty Mississippi dumps a lot of water into the Gulf, all the water is from countless contributories dumping into the Mississippi river. There are dozens of Agricultural states up river from here and tons of untreated animal waste, and who knows how many different types of fertilizers and pesticides all washing into the Gulf. Hell that's not taking into consideration all the upriver city's sewer treatment plants. Man think about all the garbage just washing down storm drains, lord knows what is in that crap, lawn fertilizers weed killers, motor oil and pet shit. This crap washes right into all these smaller rivers and it ends up dumping into the Mississippi and she dumps all this disgusting mixture into the Gulf of Mexico. This dead zone right now is 8,800 square miles; it's bigger than the state of New Jersey and my friends it is growing." Carl looked at us and smiled.

Poe was up and standing now and was looking back and forth between the three of us, he started a low bark.

"It's time we head back to the Dome of Time, said Sandra, sounds like Poe has spoken, its potty time."

"I think you are right Sandra, we are almost out of time in this trip, besides I have seen enough human waste and stupidly in the last 20 minutes to last me a long while."

Carl took out his Zippo held it in his hand. "We will have much to talk over when we get home to the Time Dome."

He clicked his lighter twice and I immediately heard the wind sound, and we were on our way back to 1974 North Carolina.

My God I said to myself, the last twenty minutes had frightened me, disgusted me and changed me forever. The shocking truth is that right now the world is being poisoned to death from dozens of different sources and directions and nobody is doing a fucking thing to change any of it. Carl is right Mr. Extinction is so very damn sneaky. ....*Why the hell not?*

Gimme Shelter
Chapter 17

The wind sound ended also most as soon as it began and we sat in the Dome of Time in the bright North Carolina sunshine.

No sooner did the shield come down that Poe took off and headed right to the brown dirt of the unplanted garden.

"Not to worry Carl, I bought a "pooper scooper" Sandra said. "Sandra I like Poe, he is a great dog, but he is your dog, I enjoy having him around but I do not deal with the technical issues, that woman is your department." Carl joked.

We three just sat in our lawn chairs and said nothing; just enjoying being back home in the Dome of Time again, as strange as this place maybe, it is our home. The silence of the Dome was broken by the Rolling Stones talking in the background. They chatted for about a minute and, I heard Keith say, "Okay let's give it a go" and the opening chorus of the song "Gimme Shelter" started to play.

"My God said Sandra of all the 100's of songs these guys have recorded over the years they pick this song to play now."

"Carl do you have any blackberry brandy with you? I asked. The Stone's song selection pushed me over the edge; I think I need a shot of "Mr. Boston."

"I never leave home without it. Black Berry Brandy is one of the basic food groups." He said flashing that grin of his. We passed the bottle between the three of us, as Carl filled the pipe with hash and lit it. I listened to the words of Gimme Shelter very closely and maybe really for the first time.

"Oooooh, the storm is threatening my very life today, if I don't get some shelter, yea I'm going to fade away. Oooooh, see the fire is sweeping down our very streets today, burning like a mad bull that lost his way. Rape and Murder are just a shot away, just a shot away. Gimmie Shelter or I'm going to fade away. Hey baby, it's just a shot away, just a shot away."

The vocals of Merry Clayton blending with Mick's had the most haunting apocalyptic sound, they shook me deeply.

I could feel every note pass though my body. Sandra spoke; you could tell the song had affected her too by the tone of her voice. "That song fits so well with what we witnessed today, I am not sure if the Stones were thinking about the end of the world when they wrote this, but boys and girls, they nailed it."

We all sat in silence just listening to the power of Mick's and Merry's voices, "Gimmie Shelter or I'm going to fade away," these words carried a strange power with them.

The song ended and we didn't move or say anything for quite a few minutes.

Sandra stood and broke the silence. "I'm going to get my bathing suit and float around in the pool for awhile. Today was such an intense day and it's not even 10 am in the morning Dome time yet. Damn I have to get wet guys, I have a lot of thinking to do." Sandra started walking towards the house. Poe zipped out of nowhere and was right next to her as she opened the door and went inside.

"Carl my friend, living with you is beyond interesting. Before I found the Dome of Time and met you I had a nice quite life, I lived alone in the North Carolina woods. I got to surf a lot as, I mean as much as I could. Man, I worked on the big ships and travelled the world and made good money, my life was not bad at all, and man I was happy.

I take a walk in the woods on my 25th birthday, run into the Dome of Time and I meet you. Then you tell me I'm the first person in all of history to find the Dome of Time and that Time Travel is my destiny. My destiny? Hell I still have not figured that one out yet. Then you tell me that the yellow Time pole glowed just so I could find the Time Dome. For some unknown reason the Time Pole wanted me to find the Dome of time."

"Sounds right so far" Carl spoke up, as he opened a Coors and handed it to me.

"Okay I'm just checking dude, I said as I continued, today is the seventh day I have been living with you in the Dome of Time, and my seventh day as a Time Traveler," as I took a big drink of ice cold Coors.

"Still sounds right on Brian," he said with that damn grin.

"Carl since I met you I have been to see the dinosaurs, I went to the moon to watch Neil Armstrong's first step on the Lunar surface. You and I went to Mars at fucking light speed. Man we three rode in an Atomic bomb blast to the edge of space. Dude, Sandra and I went surfing in the year 1111 in Hawaii twice; then we all went surfing in 1414 North Carolina and hung out with the Cape Fear Indians!

Hell I went to the D-day invasion, we saw Edgar Allan Poe dying in the gutter in 1849 Baltimore. Both intense.

Man we were 15 yards from the Rolling Stones Live, 20 years in the future in 1994 Denver. I went to a Disco show in 2017 Coney Island and I'm still not sure why. Then the three of us had Nathan's hot dogs for lunch while we orbited the earth. Hell we pretended we were a U.F.O., and waved at the people in the Space Station just for the fun of it. Man we just watched the west coast burning down; and I sat right above the Great Northern Pacific Garbage patch and Henderson Island.

Not five minutes ago I was 20 feet over the "Dead Zone".

"Carl, correct me if I am wrong but didn't you say I have 500 plus years of Time Travelling to yet to come?"

Carl looked at me and said, "Brian there are a whole lot of things I have done, but I have never had too much fun." I felt my mouth fall open in disbelief. That was by far the very last thing I expected to come out of Carl's mouth.

Carl looked at me and said. "You know Brian you have never had too much fun either. The next 500 years could prove to be very interesting, we three are going to have a fantastic time zapping around in Time."

About then Sandra came out of the house with Poe by her side, she walked up to me holding her bikini top pressed to her chest. "Brian, will you tie this damn thing up for me? I hate these things." She said as she flipped her hair out of my way.

"Come on guys she said in a coaxing voice get your trunks on, it is time to float around for awhile, we all need some head clearing time and besides our pool is 85 degrees, it feels wonderful." Sandra walked toward the pool, tossed in a very large rubber mat, dove in and climbed up on the mat. Poe was right behind her, she helped him climb up on her and he stretched out on her lap. The two of them looked so comfortable just floating in the warm pool.

"Looks like we are going swimming Carl, let's get our baggies on and float around for a while, I need to get wet and clear my head. I have a lot of thinking and soul searching to do."

As we started walking towards the house, I looked at Carl and said, "So you have never had too much fun?"

He looked at me with that damn Cheshire cat grin again.

"Brian, the three of us are going to have a blast playing around in Time, we will have 'Fun, fun, fun till Daddy takes the T-Bird Away'. You got to Love the Beach Boys, he said. Wow we can go see the "Beach Boys" live in 1965, remind me later Brian. We will catch them some place in southern California so we get the full surfer crazy effect, like totally Cowabunga dude." He grinned.

"The Beach Boys live in '65. That would be so cool; I will definitely not let you forget about going to see the Beach Boys live Carl. Now my friend, it is time to go swimming."

Wow, live Beach Boys, Carl is right. I have never had too much fun, I said to myself. *Why the hell not?*

It took me almost no time to slip on my Birdwell trunks and head out to join Sandra and Poe in the pool. I tossed in an air mat and dove in, man the water felt fantastic. I came up next to the mat and climbed on and paddled up next to Sandra. "Hey there good looking do you come here often, what sign are you?" I said to Sandra jokingly.

She reached over and held my hand, looked at me and smiled. "My sign is slippery when wet." We both started to laugh. We floated in silence for a few minutes looking up at the clear blue sky and holding hands like two teenagers.

"Brian can you believe all the crap we witnessed firsthand today? People are killing the world and nobody seems to give a damn. I never knew that things were that bad and gotten that far along, God what we saw today is not only sickening it is also so sad. It is more than sad, it is dreadful. Apocalypse is peaking around the corner at us." She had a few tears on her cheeks as she said this.

"Sandra, Carl told me something before that made me think, he said these events will happen one way or another, but by us being Time Travelers we are now being made aware of them. We are seeing them as they are happening. We now have a new outlook on the world and often it is not very pretty. Carl also said some events in time can be changed but others are in stone and cannot be altered. Let's just put everything out of our minds for awhile and enjoy floating in this nice warm water. Later when Carl gets out here and we have had a chance to chill out we will talk about what we can change and how, after all we have nothing but time. But now let's just enjoy being here together, okay?"

We held hands, floated and said nothing just lying back looking up at the light blue North Carolina sky. I felt like closing my eyes and taking a nap, this has been one long, strange and stressful day, I felt bone tired. Damn it's not even 10:30 a.m. Dome time yet.

As we laid there floating in the warm water, I could hear the Stones start recording the song "Time is on my side."

I had to wonder if time was really on our side or had the world run out of time, God I was tired and I drifted off to sleep.

Not in Kansas Anymore.
Chapter 18

I woke to the sound of Sandra's laugh, it made me smile. I was still lying on my rubber mat in the nice warm water; she and Carl were floating on the far side of the pool. I splashed some water on my face to wake up Sandra looked over and said. "Welcome back Brian, you have been asleep, we were trying to be careful and not wake you up."

I looked over and saw Sandra floating on her mat, Poe the dog was still lying across her lap. Carl was floating in his huge blow up yellow rubber duck with a straw hat on. They were both drinking a Coors; the endless cooler was floating right next to them. "Hey man Carl said, paddle over here and grab a wake up Coors, you were out like a light. Sandra is right we did not mean to wake you dude, you did look so comfortable."

"Yeah I am good at taking naps; I said I learned the art of napping while working on the big ships. One of my rules was, sleep whenever and wherever you can and work as much as possible. I loved overtime money.

Hey guys what time it is, how long was I out?"

"It's a little after noon Brian, you have been out over an hour. Carl answered. We did try to be quiet; you looked so relaxed and happy. How you feeling dude?" He asked.

"Thanks for asking Carl I feel much better, I need to close my eyes and zone out, floating in this damn warm water is so comfortable. Putting in this pool was such a good idea, thanks again Carl."

"Don't thank me Brian, this pool is here because of Sandra and her religious beliefs. You remember her telling me about how she is a California girl and that laying in the grass to tan is breaking the first Commandment of her religion."

"Thou shall only lie on the beach or by a pool to tan."

"It was something close to that, anyway, I had to take her at her word on that commandment stuff; after all she is the very first "Wowee Zoweeist" I ever met. As a matter of fact I never even heard of her religion till she brought it up, but hey any religion based on the teaching of a Frank Zappa song is okay by me. The way I looked at it I had two choices, I could zap in a swimming pool or Sandra would end up going to hell and I felt sorry for the poor Devil so I zapped in a pool. I really don't think that Satan is ready for Sandra."

That statement started us all laughing, after all that was witnessed by us today we all needed a good hard laugh. We just lay in the warm pool for a long while, giggling like little kids and enjoyed being alive.

At long last Sandra spoke up. "Brian, before you woke up Carl and I were talking. We decided to give ourselves a while to chill and try to avoid talking about everything we were exposed to today, kind of like take the day off and take it easy. Lay around in the Time Dome or maybe go surfing again this afternoon. Later this evening we are going to grill up a big batch of cheeseburgers on our new Bar B.Q. How does that sound?" She asked.

"What, we are not going to have fish sandwiches for dinner?" I joked. That comment cracked us all up again.

The Stones were back in the studio and playing around, picking a few notes and talking back and forth, could hear Keith Richards count off 1, 2, next thing we heard was, "The joint was rocking going around and around, just reeling and a rocking what a crazy sound, they never stopped rocking till the moon went down."

"Live Stones you got to love it, it sure is nice being home again said Carl. I do love our sound system."

Carl was right about needing to take head clearing time when you Time Travel and how nice it was to come back to the Dome and chill.

Dude I now live way out in the North Carolina woods in the Dome of Time. The Dome that is surrounded by millions of little white Ziplinks who crashed here in their 1949 ford space ship 1000 years ago. Dude we can hear the Rolling Stones recording live as it is happening.

We drink Coors beer from an igloo cooler that never runs out of Coors. A cooler that was a gift from space travelling Big Mac eating fish people called the Norsins.

There is a Yellow Time pole just sitting there in the middle of the Dome that also happens to be the exact center of the universe. That damn Yellow pole has every event that has ever happened or will happen in all of time stuffed inside of it. Man I live in an old wooden house that sits inside the Dome of Time. I like living here, it is a very comfortable home, and it feels right.

I share the house with two very interesting people. I enjoy living with both Sandra and Carl, I feel very comfortable with them. It was like we three belonged together. It is fun being with one or both of them. I must admit it was more fun being with Sandra but not much of a surprise there. Talking about a bonus, Carl is a great cook and he loves to cook, sorry mom, I have never eaten this well in my life. Hell we even own a pet, a little black time travelling dog named Poe, who we found in the gutter in 1974 Baltimore. He is one happy, well behaved, smart dog; you have just got to love him. Tonight we are going to grill up a bunch of cheeseburgers, lay back drink ice cold Coors, and take it easy by the pool and let our minds clear.

Dude I feel like I am living in a re-run of "Leave it to Beaver."

Man this Dome is going to be my home for the next 500 plus years to come. No matter how weird the place is, it is home and Carl is right it did feel good to be home and shut out the world for awhile.

Damn straight Brian, you know tomorrow there will be some very heavy subjects raising their ugly heads, but tonight you are home and are going to enjoy a nice quite night and relax with your best friends.

Heard It through the Grapevine
Chapter 19

It was very early morning, the sun was just coming up, there was enough light in Sandra's room to make out her face lying next to me in her new bed. She felt soft and warm, I could feel her slowly breathing, and she is an outstandingly beautiful woman.

I enjoyed just watching her sleeping. I rolled over and there on her wall was a big "Saturday Night Fever" poster hanging next to the portrait that Vincent Van Gough had painted of her. She must have time zapped back to Coney Island at some point to pick up a poster. No surprise there, she told us she thought John Travolta was cute and she wanted a poster so she went and got one. Sandra is a hell of an independent woman. I'm surprised she didn't track down John and get him to autograph it for her. Yep I could see Sandra doing just that. "Hello John, I'm a big fan, would you please autograph this poster I picked up forty years in the future." I had to chuckle to myself, it sounded silly, but at the same time it was so possible and it did sound so much like something Sandra would do. She is a handful.

I closed my eyes and took a deep breath; my mind was already racing, so much happened yesterday and I knew the events of yesterday are going to be the topic of conversation today. I am not sure if I'm mentally prepared to face all that ugliness again, but I knew I had no choice in the matter. Sandra was dead set on sending the world a wakeup call and Carl had told us we needed to talk about it. I was all Gung ho about saving the world at one point yesterday, but the more I saw of the giant apocalyptic mess, the less convinced I became that there was anything we could do to wake up the world.

Yesterday had been a very intense day in my life. I had been dragged from the blissful ignorance of my life in 1974 to the reality of the world of 2017 all within the space of two hours Dome time. I had been slapped in the face with 40 plus years of incredible waste and gross stupidity. I didn't just hear about these things, I saw them up close and personal. I am not sure what is going to take place in the next few hours but I'm sure whatever it is it will rip at my guts again. For now I'm going to put these things out of my mind and lay here and be so very thankful for it. I am comfortable, I am warm, I was safe and I was lying next to the most incredible woman I had ever met. I dozed off again.

I felt Sandra kiss me and heard "Good morning Brian."

I opened my eyes it was much brighter in the room and I could see everything very well now. I rolled over and said "Good morning Baby."

"I had a nice time last night grilling burgers and lying around and taking it easy was a good idea, we needed a time out after yesterday's events. Oh by the way I see you went back and got a "Saturday Night Fever poster."

"Yeah yesterday was a very intense day, we needed some zone out time, last night helped clear my head and yes Brian I went and got myself a poster. I told you I thought John was cute, besides he's got a real sexy butt, you're not jealous are you Brian?" she laughed.

"Jealous? Come here woman and I will show you jealous." Making love with Sandra early in the morning is an incredible way to start the day, she felt so right. Honestly it feels like Time stops when we are together. I lose myself in her warmth, her smell and softness of her haunting hair.

We needed each other, it was not being said between the two of us but it was there. A warm deep feeling that neither of us could deny or at this point either of us would admit. I am really falling hard for this woman and I can see no reason not to. We lay there for the longest time not wanting this time together to end.

"Baby, she said. We have got to get up, take a shower and catch up with Carl. You know he is going to cook a big breakfast for us and after that who knows what he has in mind and where the hell we will end up. Time travelling with Carl is to say the least very interesting, come on Brian move your cute butt babe."

I loved Sandra's shower, it so big and bright. It took us no time to get ourselves together and head out and look for Carl.

As soon as we walked down the hall we could hear the stereo blasting out the song, "Ape Man" by the Kinks.

"I'm an ape-man an ape man an ape, ape, ape –man, I don't feel safe in this world no more and I don't want to die in a nuclear war. I want to sail away to a distant shore and make like a Ape-Man." Sandra and I stopped and looked at each other. I had to wonder if that song was a preview of things to come today.

I heard Sandra ask above the music "Hey Carl where are you?"

"Out here on the front porch guys." He answered. Sandra and I walked out on the pouch. It was an outstanding North Carolina morning everything looked so alive. The air smells so clean and of course the sky was a light blue, so far this is a fantastic day. We said. "Good morning Carl" and he replied "Morning."

Sandra and I sat down in our rocking chairs and we all sat just rocking saying nothing for a few minutes just enjoying the early morning.

"I have been waiting for you two to get up, so I could cook us up some breakfast. I figured you guys needed to sleep in today; I hope you guys are hungry, because I'm starved. There is coffee and hash in the kitchen come on in and get a cup of coffee and let's do a bowl of hash. I will whip up some breakfast, okay with you two?"

"Sounds like a plan Sandra said as she stood up, coffee sounds like a great idea, but then again so does hash, come on Brian."

I caught myself almost saying the words "Yes dear" but I managed to get a grip on myself, and say "Okay" instead.

I love this kitchen always so bright and clean, and comfortable. Sandra and I filled our mugs with coffee and I lit the pipe. I took a hit of hash, yes so far this is a very good day indeed, I thought to myself.

"You guys mind setting the table while I cook up a big omelet for us. There is always clean plates and silver wear. I never wash dishes I just zap them back to a time when they were clean." He just grinned at us.

Sandra and I looked at each other, man that sounds so damn strange. Zapping the dishes back to a time they were clean? We never know if Carl is putting us on or not, but then again zapping dishes around is no stranger than anything else in my life and knowing Carl, *why the hell not?*

We ate breakfast off our Time zapped clean plates without saying much of anything; we were all hungry and ate our fill. The omelet was a work of art; damn I am glad Carl loves to cook because I love eating his creations.

We sat drinking coffee and smoking hash, still not saying much, listening to the Kink's LP playing in the background. It was like we all knew the topic of conversation would be intense today and we were all putting it off for as long as we could. "Dudes stick the dishes in the sink I will zap them later. Let's go outside and sit on the porch awhile." Carl suggested.

"Sounds like a great idea Carl said Sandra, oh and thanks for breakfast it was super."

"Yeah Carl breakfast was great, thanks man." I added. We walked out on the pouch and could hear the Stones talking in the background, and the song "Down Home Girl" started to play in the Dome.

"Lord I swear the perfume you wear is made out of turnip greens, and every time I kiss you girl it tastes like pork and beans."

"I love our sound system said Carl, music makes it all worthwhile sometimes and those boys can rock out."

I pulled my rocker up closer to the rail so I could put my feet up, Carl and Sandra did the same.

We sat listening to "Down Home Girl" with our feet on the rail looking out at the North Carolina pines and the clear blue sky. I heard Mick sing a great verse, "Girl the dress you wear is made out of fiberglass, every time you move like that I got to go to Sunday mass, oh girl you are so down home."

I broke the silence between us by jumping right into it.

"Carl you are so right about needing head clearing time when you Time Travel. Yesterday in two hours you introduced me to global warming and showed me a world on fire. I saw poison water and an earth choking in plastics. I needed to come back here and zone out for awhile just to let it all sink in. It's a lot to take in all at once and the best part is I know it's not over yet, there is a lot more to come. I see no reason for putting this off any longer, let's talk. Okay with you guys?" I asked.

Sandra spoke up. "I'm with Brian what we saw yesterday was nothing short of apocalyptic and Brian's right it all happened so fast. It was a huge slap in the face by a thing called reality. It was like reality was shouting at us; here I am take a good look at me. Dude, we got a real good look at reality."

Okay guys Carl began. "This is a huge problem but the solution starts in small steps. Little steps like bend down pick up trash and put it in the garbage can. It is not hard to do and anyone can do it, now comes the hard part getting people to do it. Carl's voice was firm. Little steps man just a bunch of little steps, like get rid of plastic bags, great place to start, but once again you got to get people to do it."

"Ah, getting people to take the first step is the hard part. Little steps start with people saying no more, enough is enough; don't buy certain items till the manufacturers get it right."

"Dude, money talks, boycott and you would see change, and the change will happen real damn fast. Little steps man. Little steps have a habit of turning into bigger steps."

Carl then asked. "You guys want a Coors?" We both said. "Yes." He opened three and hand us a Coors each. "Carl keep going, you were talking about big steps." Sandra said as she took her Coors from him.

Carl went on. "Ah but the bigger steps have to be taken on as a joint effort by the entire world, do you really think that will happen? Shit, here are the facts. If all the countries of the world do not take a firm stance on certain global issues, nothing else will matter. All the squabbles going on between the different countries in the world right now will add up to less than nothing if the earth dies. Shit, a lot of these countries are being financed by the very people who are fucking things up."

Check this out he said. "Starting right now, if every developed nation in the world recycled every bit of the plastic they produce it would barely make a dent in the total amount of plastic waste that is being dumped by dozens of underdeveloped countries right this second."

"Are there some magic words that will make all of the powers that be understand this is not a game, this is forever?" Carl had the most intense look in his eyes.

He then got a huge smile on his face and said. "Hey, Sandra, Brian you know what? We could always forget all this save the world crap. Sure thing dudes we can just say fuck it and go back to buzzing around in time having a ton of fun. We could have endless adventures and not worry about anything. We could surf all over the world throughout all of time, man we can have a real blast. We can zap around in Time and have way too much fun."

He took one look at Sandra's face and added "Or maybe not?"

Totally Dude!
Chapter 20

"Carl, there is no way in hell I'm going to let this slide, there has to be something we can do to make changes. You're right about small steps and one person with a good idea and making it work, we can do this." Sandra insisted. No way I can just go play around in time and have fun while I know the world is being killed. Hell you showed me this mess Carl there has to be a reason why. I know you pretty well Carl. In your roundabout way, you always have a reason why. You started this man, we are not going to walk away without at least trying to bring about some kind of global changes." Sandra was very firm in this statement.

"Look Sandra we need a real good plan. We are up against huge odds; use of throw away plastic items like bottles and bags has gone up 600% since 1975. First we have to get the world to ban the manufacture of non bio- degradable and non recyclable plastics and second we have to get them to clean up the mess that's out there. It's not that easy to pull off."

"Some of the countries that are drowning in plastics cannot even provide basic service to their population. We are talking about clean running water, sewers and garbage collection that is nonexistent. Man we are talking about the downright nastiest slums you can imagine, where people are born into a world of garbage. Places where people eat a few feet from where they shit. These people live in a world of filth, smothered by single use plastic."

"You both know where the Philippines are and you both know the capital is Manila, once called the Pearl of the Orient. Check this out; the Pasig river, the main river that flows into Manila bay has been declared biologically dead since 1990. Think about that for a few seconds; the river is fucking dead, nothing can live in it. There are dozens of rivers up stream that dump into the Pasig; the plastic in some of these rivers is so thick a person can walk across them on plastic. No shit dude, so thick it will support the weight of a man. When monsoon season hits all that plastic crap washes right down the river and ends up in the Pacific Ocean."

"We are talking about Manila; I have been there a few times in the past. The turn of the century Manila was a beautiful city. I had a lot of fun in Manila over the years, but now it has a slum called "Aroma" and another named "Happyland."

"Babies are born in Aroma and live their whole life in filth. The people who live there pick through the plastic waste for any plastic with a recyclable value, they are lucky to make $100 a month. It is not like there are not people out there who would be more than happy to clean up the mess, if they made a living wage doing so."

"The problem is a lot of plastic has no value; it cannot be recycled so it is tossed out and piles up.

Now; if they put a value on all plastic, recyclable or not, the plastic would be cleaned up.

Dude, a worldwide tax of only a few cents on every pound of plastic produced would raise billions of dollars a year. That money could be used to pay for a worldwide clean up of the mess, or at least get a good start on getting the problem under control."

"Now the fun part, getting the plastic industry to pay up. I told you this would not be easy Sandra."

"Carl we just can't give in, what the hell could be more fun than changing the whole world? Carl we have to think of this as a Big Game, you, me and Brian take on the whole fucking world. We are smart enough and have time travelling on our side, we can do this. Let's go for it, us against the powers that be."

"Carl you can be so damn sneaky, think of it as us pulling a big joke on the world. Ha-ha, we made you ass holes save the world and you didn't even know we did it, *so there*." She was laughing as she said this.

Carl said, "I love the idea of us pulling the wool over the world eyes Sandra but we are dealing with the likes of China. It is a paranoid mess of a place to begin with. They are the world's biggest polluter and not just plastics."

"Hell, you are talking about a country that burns so much coal, the sky is black and you cannot see 25 yards. The people have to wear masks in order to breathe."

He kept talking. "Ah, but China is making lots of money and after all that's what counts."

"They are a prime example of a country with lots of brand new shiny things that kill and no real plastic disposal methods and they are doing almost nothing to control air pollution."

Carl leaned over and grabbed 3 cans of Coors out of the cooler, opened them, and handed one to Sandra and one to me. He took a long drink and started talking again.

"Damn woman, last year Coca-Cola made over 120 billion plastic bottles, with Pepsi and other bottling companies not far behind. Until you can get the source of the pollution to change its packaging you are just banging your head against the wall. Woman you are talking about taking on the most populated county in the world and Coke and that's just the tip of the iceberg."

"Shame on us if we can't outfox the likes of China and Coke." Sandra was laughing, pretty hard when she asked me. "What you think Brian?"

"I don't think the powers that be have a chance against you Sandra." I replied. "It is a going to take a lot of cunning on our part, but we do have time on our side. Changing the world sounds like a great Game to play, I'm in."

"I also think we should go surfing for a few hours and let this idea of us out foxing the world sink in. I got just the spot to go surfing picked out and on the right time and date.

Check it out, I want to go back to Oahu to a surf spot I know called "Queens."

"Pretty waves, sandy bottom, clear blue water, a great place for Carl. It has a nice inside break, and hell people take their kids there to learn to surf. Best part is there are some super nice outside waves for you and me Sandra; some really great nose riding waves, we are bringing our long boards. You guys will love this place."

"Plus it is right next to Diamondhead, what a super view and we will be the only ones there. I have a great date and time picked out. We will go back there at 12:34 p.m. on May 6, in the year 789. Get it guys? 123456789. Is that not too cool or what?"

"Surfing sounds like a great idea Brian." They both said at the same time.

Sandra looked at me and said "Brian only you could come up with going surfing on 123456789, I love It." She leaned over and kissed me and whispered in my ear, "I love the color of your hair babe."

"Thanks" was all I could say, that woman can leave me speechless.

"Surfing in Hawaii sounds like so much fun," said Carl. We can level 3 back in time. We will bring our boards, the lawn chairs, endless cooler and the hash. This is going to be so much fun surfing in Hawaii in the year 789."

"We cannot forget clean water and a bowl for Poe and his long rope so he can walk around. I know there is plenty of shade for him to lie in; he is going to have a blast sniffing around in the jungle."

"Hey Poe you want to go to Hawaii?" Sandra asked him. Poe was up and spinning around, with little jumps and hops. "I think he wants to go to Hawaii," she exclaimed.

"Okay boy and girls let's get ourselves together and go to Hawaii. Hey guys do you remember that Beach Boy's song that kind of goes like this?" Carl stated to sing.

"Hawaii. Hawaii, straight to Hawaii. Honolulu, Waikiki, do you want to come along with me?"

"Great song, hey man we are going surfing in Hawaii, his grin was huge. I will look up the number and lock it into my Zippo. We will get changed, stuff some things into a bag and off we go to Hawaii. Wow I was just thinking the last time I was in Hawaii was in 1962 when we watched the atomic bomb Starfish Prime detonate. Damn we did that only a few days ago." Carl shook his head. "Time loves to fuck with your head."

"That is something I will never forget Sandra replied, but this trip will help make up for it."

"Hey Carl, speaking of the Beach Boys you said we can catch them live in 1965, don't forget." I said.

"Wow the Beach Boys live in 1965 what a trip added Sandra. I can't wait that will be so much fun, don't you dare forget Carl, wow the Beach Boys live."

It took us no time at all to get changed, grab our boards and meet up by the time pole. We sat in our lawn chairs; of course the endless cooler was right next to Carl's chair.

"You guys ready?" Sandra had Poe by his collar; she and I both said 'Ready!' "Crap" said Carl.

"Sandra, I want to bring your lap top with us; it is hooked up to the time pole and will work in any time period. While we are hanging out in 789 Hawaii we may want to look up information about the global warming mess."

"Good thinking Carl said Sandra; I will run back to the house and get it. She started back toward the house with a skip, Poe was right next to her, she was back in no time, and she sat down, held Poe next to her, looked at Carl and said. "Let's go Carl, time is wasting. To Hawaii my man." Sandra and I pushed the green buttons on our time travel watches.

Carl clicked his Zippo twice, the wind sound went on for a few seconds and we are sitting on the beach in Hawaii at precisely 123456789, just because we can.

So what do ya think?
Chapter 21

"Wow! My God look at those waves; they are perfect, 4 to 6 footers, long rights with a nice light off shore breeze and nobody else is out. Perfect, just perfect, this is a dream, Sandra was definitely excited. Can you believe this? We are sitting on Waikiki beach in 123456789.

I love time travel, exclaimed Sandra in a loud voice. We have this island to ourselves, there is not a person for 1000's of miles."

"Man, Diamondhead is right there. Think about this guys, 1173 years from now we will be sitting right over Diamondhead watching man made death in the Starfish Prime atomic bomb test. Wow, you are right Carl we just did that five days ago, time travel is so damn strange." Sandra said.

She let go of Poe who ran up to the nearest sand crab to say hello, the crab wanted no part of it and let Poe know it. Poe let out a little yelp and shook his head and slowly walked back to Sandra, looking back at the crab a few times. "Don't stick your nose where it don't belong Poe, she looked at his nose, no harm done." She said.

"Guys, I said, it turns out that 1173 years in the future just a few days before the Starfish Prime bomb test in 1962, I went surfing for the first time in my life right here. I was 12 years old."

"My dad had been transferred to Hickam Air Force base and the military put us up in a hotel a few blocks from the beach till we found a place to live. I bugged the crap out of my dad to let me go surfing, I am sure I was a real pain in the ass about it. He asked around and someone told him to take me to "Queens," it was a great beginners spot to surf. My dad rented a board right here on this very beach, heck we are sitting just about where the surf board rental stand will be. Anyway he rented a board for me, man it was a great big log of a surf board with a fixed wooden skeg, the board weighed a ton. No matter I was so sure I was going to be the world's best surfer. I had no idea of what I was doing, hell I had never seen a surf board till a few days before this and I had definitely never been on one before."

"When you are 12 years old you have a different outlook about reality, I was going to be the greatest surfer in the world no doubt about it. I paddled out, tried to catch my first wave and I played "U" boat and the board went deep under water nose first. It flew up in the air came back down and the skeg hit me. It put a huge black and blue mark on the side my upper leg. Man I could hardly walk. The first wave I paddled into was one of the worst wipeouts I have ever taken in my life, man it hurt like hell."

"So then what happened, Brian?" Sandra asked.

"They had to chop my leg off and I never surfed again in my life," I said laughing. That statement cracked up both Carl and Sandra. "Na I paddled right back out again and rode the next wave right up to the beach. Riding that wave was the end of any chance of me going to Yale. The water had become my life with that one ride. Now almost 1200 years in the past I'm going surfing at the very place it all started. Damn time travel can be so damn strange."

"Didn't I just say that?" Asked Sandra as she poked me in my ribs. I just looked at her and smiled.

"Why don't you paddle out Sandra? Man you will be the first person to ever surf in Hawaii again, Sandra you were the first person to surf in the Atlantic, now the first person to surf in Hawaii, you get around girl. I will get Poe all squared away and then work some with Carl on his surfing. I want to show him how to paddle out and how to roll under. Once I get him up to speed I will paddle out and join you."

"Brian this is unreal we are surfing in Hawaii for the third time, I really love time traveling." She said with a huge grin. She picked up her board, leaned over and kissed me and said, "I love the color of your hair babe."

She walked down to the water's edge and knelt down to wax her board as I held Poe's collar. She started to paddle out, looked back and yelled. "This water is beautiful, don't be too long Brian."

Carl started to sing that Beach Boys song again. "Hawaii straight to Hawaii, Honolulu, Waikiki, do you want to come along with me?" Truth be told, he had a nice singing voice.

"Dude I said, let's get Poe comfortable and out of our way and I will teach you more about surfing."

We found a nice palm tree with good shade, tied Poe's long rope to it, filled his bowl with water, petted his head and told him to be a good dog. I looked back at him and he was walking around smelling everything; his tail wagging. He was having a good time exploring.

"Come on Carl, grab your board I have a few things I am going to show you. These waves have a lot more power than the ones at Top Sail beach."

Sandra was paddling into her first wave, she pulled a hard bottom turn, climbed to the top of the wave, and she came back down walking her board for a super long nose ride. We could hear her yell, "I fucking love time travel, man did you guys see that ride?" She was paddling back out before we could say anything.

"Hey Carl I got a few things I want to show you so you can get out past the shore break. Let's grab your board we will not go out very deep, I will demonstrate how you do it, okay?"

"Brian this means a lot to me, you taking the time to teach me how to surf. I really love surfing. I can't wait to be able to out surf you and Sandra." He said with a big grin.

"There you go again Carl; you have such a great imagination! Out surfing me *and* Sandra? Ha! I scoff at you." I said laughing.

"Dude, while we are alone. Do you think there is any chance in hell we can make the world aware of what the fuck is going on with global warming and the plastic waste? Sandra is bound and determined to change things and you know how she is and we are living in the middle of it. Man is there anything we can do to make changes Carl?"

"Brian it is like this, we cannot undo what has already happened, it is a done deal, however can we make some changes in future events. Now, how we will go about getting our point across is open for debate. We have to make enough people want to unite and deal with these problems. Brian we have much to talk over, but now let's go surfing after all we are in Hawaii."

"Give me a straight up answer Carl can we pull this off?"

"To tell you the truth Brian, I think of this as a giant Game and the other side has no idea it is even being played. Yes, I think we can make a difference in the world, but it will not be fast and it will not be easy and I have no idea how yet. Now can we go surfing?" He asked.

"Thanks man I needed to hear that Carl, and I patted him on his back. Now let's get to surfing."

I spent about 15 minutes showing Carl how to paddle out and how to roll under white water. I said have fun dude take it slow and do not play "U" boat okay? I going to paddle out with Sandra, yell if you need any help. Kind of keep an eye on Poe, have fun Carl." And I was off and paddling out into beautiful Hawaiian waves in the year 789 A.D. *Why the hell not?*

It took me no time at all to paddle out to where Sandra was surfing. I watched her get a great ride as I was on my way out. "Hey, nice ride babe I said. Save some waves for me."

"Forget it; get your own waves buddy, she laughed. God I love this break, it was like it was made to nose ride." She was as giddy as a little kid with a candy buzz.

"I surfed here a bunch in the early 60's I said; I hung five for the first time right here on this break. Ya want to see me hang five again?" I joked at her.

We traded wave after wave. I was no longer aware of the outside world, the waves and the water consumed me, they became my world, it is one of those things if you do not surf you will never understand. This zone out went on for hours; it was damn haunting, a surfing trance.

Sandra spoke first, "Brian we died and went to surfer heaven. I cannot believe these waves, this whole place is *"Breathtaking."* There are those words again.

"Let's paddle in and check on Carl and Poe, what do you think?" I asked.

"Good thinking, hey Brian I am glad I met you." She splashed some water at me, turned and paddled into a nice 4 foot wave.

Well that took me by surprise I said to myself as I got a big grin on my face. I was right behind her on the very next wave. We rode all the way up to the beach and picked up our boards and walked up the beach toward Carl, who was sitting in his lawn chair drinking a Coors. He had let Poe off his line and Poe came running down to met Sandra, talking to her in soft little barks. We walked up to Carl and sat down in our lawn chairs.

"Did you have fun surfing Carl?" I asked.

"Dude I kick myself for not taking up surfing years ago, it's not like I didn't have the time. Hey you guys want a cold Coors?" He asked. We both said "Yes." He opened two beers and handed one to each of us.

We are sitting on Waikiki beach in the year 789 drinking ice cold Coors, right next to Diamondhead watching the crystal clear surf. We are completely alone, not a sound of man to be heard.

They went that away……!
Chapter 22

We sat on this undiscovered beach watching the day slowly moving on to its ultimate end of night. At least a half an hour passed before anyone of us spoke. We opened a fresh Coors once in a while but said nothing.

Sandra stood up and turned so she was looking at Carl and me. "This is absolutely an amazing place" she said spreading her arms out. "Maybe you are right Carl why should we get ourselves all worked up about trying to save the world? Man we could spend our lives' surfing great places like this every day for the next 500 plus years? The goings on in the world mean nothing to us.

If we don't like what's going on we can zap someplace new. We can avoid all the problems and troubles and just zap throughout time and have a blast." The look on her face suddenly changed to a very puzzled look.

"My God did that really come out of my mouth? Sorry guys I was overcome by the Ape-man syndrome." She started to laugh pretty hard.

Carl and I looked at each other for a few seconds and broke out laughing. "You had me concerned there Sandra said Carl; I was worried you had been brain washed by the Waikiki beach karma. Glad you are back Sandra."

"Yeah babe you had me worried too, I added. Running around in time sounds like a ton of fun, but we all know you are going to try and save the world Sandra."

"You two are right. I would kick myself if I didn't follow through on the saving the world thing. It is just so peaceful and quite here it almost hypnotizes you, like it's telling me hey kick back and enjoy life, nothing to worry about, but hey I'm back now." She said grinning.

"Look guys, I have been thinking about us putting a plan together, first we have to have a list of priorities. We can sit around the kitchen table and throw out ideas and get an outline going, then decide the best course of action.

The second thing is we do not talk about this "Game" anyplace but in the dome. I want to be able to do just what we are doing now, get away from everything and take deep breaths. Oh, one other thing. We now refer to saving the world as "The Game." Okay with you guys?" She asked with that intense Sandra look in her eyes.

Carl and I took one look at Sandra, the only possible reply was "Yes Sandra."

"Hey guys let's check out my lap top and make sure it is going to work in any time period. We can look up some fun stuff, just to check it out." Sandra was grinning and already was sitting with the lap top out.

"Sandra, I will have you know I connected the lap top to the time pole myself, I know for a fact it works, said Carl looking a little annoyed. One thing I know very well is Time. Make sure it works Sandra? Ye of little faith. So you don't think I know what I'm doing? Thanks a lot."

"I'm sorry Carl I did not mean it to sound like you don't know what you are doing, I am just excited we are 1200 years in the past and we have internet. Hell we are sitting on Waikiki beach 1200 years in the past and I have internet, this is simply amazing. She had a big smile as she turned on her lap top and said "Here's Johnny," and the damn thing came to life.

"Dudes I said looking at them, a few days ago I lived in 1974. To me a computer is something a half a city block long, that makes popping and clicking sounds and is top secret and owned and run by the Pentagon or the F.B.I.

A computer is something I see in grade "B" science fiction movies. Getting my mind around the fact that Sandra is totally accustomed to dealing with a device that she can carry with one hand and she grew up using this thing on a daily basis is just one more item I will have to deal with. But right now I am going to sit and watch. Carl you told me how computers had become an everyday fact of life, but being told something and seeing it for the first time are two way different things."

She clicked a button on the key board and a photo of a wave popped up on the little TV screen.

"That picture is called a screen saver Brian, all I have to do is type in something we want to check out and the computer will bring up a bunch of what is called web sites. We can click on one or more of them and get all kinds of information to pop up on the screen; they show photos and movies about what ever subject you type in. What do you want to check out Brian?" asked Sandra.

"Let me see if I understand this Sandra, all you have to do is type something in and it appears right in front of us on that little TV thing? This I want to see."

"Okay. Sandra type in Diamond Head, seeing how we are sitting right next to it. Let's look it up and get the history and details of Diamond Head."

"I like the way you think Brian." She started to type in Diamond Head, pushed a button and I was looking at a photo of Diamond Head, I looked over my shoulder and there was the real thing just sitting there. All I could say was "Wow!"

"Welcome to the world of computers Brian," she leaned over and kissed me.

Once again I had been yanked out of 1974 and introduced to the future in the blink of an eye. Ah, but I could see something very good coming out of my introduction to computers, I could tell this was going to be extremely interesting and it was going to be a lot of fun too. Oh boy I'm going to have a bunch of fun playing with computers, oh goodie a new toy.

Why the hell not? I said to myself.

"Carry on Sandra I want to watch and learn. I kind of nudged her a little. Fill me in on this lap top thing woman, I have to be able to use a computer by myself."

Carl got up and said, "Look you two mess around on the computer, you bring Brian up to speed Sandra, I'm going surfing. You don't need my help and besides we are in 789 Hawaii and the surf is "bitchin," you like that word Brian? I looked up 1960's surfer terms."

He picked up his board, started down toward the water, yelled "Cowabunga" and paddled out.

I turned back to Sandra, "Sandra what about Diamond Head? Show me how this thing works."

She typed in Diamond Head's history and there it was in front my face. Everything I could ever want to know about Diamond Head, it was sitting right there. No going to the library, no research, just type in the right question and you got your answer in a flash.

"I feel like a fucking caveman Sandra, show me more women. I need to know everything about how this thing works. Man I want one of my own to play with, oh goodie goodie gum drops a new toy, I love fun stuff."

Sandra was very patient with me and took her time showing me how to use this little magic box called the computer, the more I learned the more I wanted to know.

It was just starting to get dark when Carl paddled in and walked up with his board under his arm.

"Hey I saw you get some real nice rides Carl."

"Thanks Sandra. I'm getting this surfing down, I love it."

"Hey you two guys have been playing with the lap top for over an hour now. So what do you think Brian?"

"Carl we have to get a computer hooked up in the house, Sandra told me they make computers called desk tops. They have printers so you can make copies of what you are looking at. They come with real big screens. Dude I have to have one of those big critters." I said.

"Yeah Brian we can do that, hell maybe we will hook up a couple of real big computers for us to play with, no big deal he said. I'm glad you enjoy playing with the lap top, once again you have jumped forward 40 years in a few hours. You have got to be having fun Brian."

"Carl, I see no choice in the matter, it is going to keep happening, I may as well be having a good time doing it." I answered

"Hey Carl, Sandra asked, as long as we are out picking up electric toys for the house how about we get a big microwave oven?" She said looking at him with those big green eyes of hers.

"You know Sandra I been thinking about getting one of those new fangled do dads," he said in an old timey voice.

"Hey Carl she went on, I know you said no before but how about we pick up a state of the arts big flat screen TV with all the whistle and bows, I mean a huge one?" She said still batting her green eyes.

"Come on Carl it will be fun having TV. We can pretend to be a normal American household we can eat dinner watching the boob tube. Wow we can time zap back to the 1950's and pick up a bunch of TV dinners." By now she was laughing pretty hard. "My dad told me about a thing called a 'TV' table, check it out, you eat your TV dinner off them, we can get matching ones." She was really laughing hard now.

Carl shook his head. "Woman you love to push my buttons. Sandra if you only knew how much I hate TV but I know you very well woman and you will bug me though out all of time till I break down and get television hooked up in the dome. Sandra we are sitting on the beach in ancient Hawaii and you bring up television, I rest my case."

"Sandra you are so fucking stubborn. Okay we will get TV hooked up, maybe more than one, but you pick them out, zap them to the dome and I will hook then up."

He changed the subject "Hey Sandra is "I love Lucy" still on? He asked. I liked Fred Mertz, I think he was way ahead of his time, a real trend setter and a very snappy dresser."

Sandra and I looked at each other, Fred Mertz a trend setter, and a snappy dresser? Carl definitely has his own way of looking at things.

I always knew Carl would end up giving into Sandra sooner or later about hooking up TV, like I said before it was just a matter of time and Sandra has plenty of that.

"Carl you are the big brother I never had. You are such a dear, this makes me so very happy, she said. And yes, you can still catch I love Lucy reruns."

"You are such a con artist Sandra, but I am really glad having television makes you happy woman."

Then he went on, "okay everyone take a look around and make sure we got everything we came with. Grab Poe Sandra," and he clicked the Zippo six times. We heard the wind sound and we were sitting back in the time dome.

We had been surfing half of the day in 789 Hawaii and been gone one minute dome time. As soon as we landed I could hear the Stones playing in the back ground, "you can't catch me, if you get too close I'm gone like a cool breeze." Man I love time travel.

Who's on First?
Chapter 23

"Boys and girls that surfing trip to Hawaii was a great idea. We can do this every day, surf warm water, beautiful waves and have the place to ourselves. There are all kinds of surf spots we can visit long before they are ever discovered and we can surf all day if we wanted to. There are a whole lot of things I have done but I never had too much fun, Carl was glowing as he said this. I really liked surfing in Hawaii and he started to sing "Dreams come true in blue Hawaii." Hey Brian do you remember that Elvis movie from 1961 Blue Hawaii? It was a big deal back then since Hawaii had just become the 50th state, a big plug at the time coming from Elvis himself."

"Carl, I think I saw it in the movie theater when I was a kid, my folks would drop me off at the Saturday matinee with 50 cents for candy and they would show movies all day long, it was a plot to get rid of the kids for a few hours."

"Hey Carl I'll have you know I'm a big Elvis fan, myself, I have seen all his movies at least twice. I own a bunch of his CD's and I think he has a cute ass," Sandra said as she poked me in the ribs.

"Hey Sandra, what is a CD?" I asked, both Carl and Sandra said at the same time "we will explain later Brian." They always say that and I am still waiting to find out what "MTV" and "Why Fly" are. I can now add CD's to that list. No matter I have lots of time.

"No fooling are you really an Elvis fan Sandra?" I asked her. She looked at me and said "don't you step on my blue suede shoes," and started to laugh.

"There is a famous scene in that movie where Elvis is singing on the steps going down to Hanauma bay. A big bay that is sheltered from the ocean by a few sets of reefs that kept the water in the bay calm and crystal clear, a great place to snorkel on a beautiful reef. Carl went on, I just read up on the place, well boys and girls, by the year 2017 part of that reef is bleached out and about 10% has died. Some of the dead coral has algae growing on it. It is a State park, so they have a lot of resources at their disposal, but no matter it is slowly being transformed by global warming."

"Carl, when I was a kid I would spend hours floating around in Hanauma bay. Back in the early 60's if you went mid week there was almost nobody in the water. I bugged the hell out my dad about a facemask, fins and a snorkel so I could skin dive there. Man the coral was unbelievable colors and the little fish would swim right up to you. I once spent an hour floating in that glass clear water watching a sea cucumber two feet under me crawl across the sandy bottom. Man that place was a dream to a 13 year boy. God I cannot believe it is dying."

"Yep pollution and global warming is killing off reefs all over the world and this place is no different. Check this out, some sunscreens are helping to kill off the reefs. This crap, Oxybenzone, found in sun screen is a threat to marine life. Yep, all the reefs around the world are going fast. 56 years after they filmed Blue Hawaii, what you once knew is now slowly dying Brian." Carl said as he shook his head.

"Hell the Great Barrier Reef is over 1,400 miles long, can be seen from space, and by 2017 it has lost about half its coral. I read some reports about the demise of coral around the world and the number one factor is climate change. The water is getting warmer and the coral cannot adjust to the sudden changes in water temperature. Add in marine pollution, ocean acidification, and disease and there go the reefs. Dude, by the year 2030 over 90 % of the reefs in the world are going to be endangered from human activities and climate change; by 2050 every reef in the world will be in danger.

Man, there are places in the world where Dynamite fishing is still used. Crap that is nothing compared to cyanide fishing, talking about 150,000 kg a year dumped in the water and that's just in the Philippines. Everyplace you look you can see the earth dying. It's just a matter of getting the people in this world to realize that once it's gone there ain't no coming back. I look over my shoulder and Mr. Extinction has a big grin on his face." Carl sounded pretty grim as he spoke.

"Man, just think what's going to happen to all those little islands in the Caribbean that depend on tourists to make a living. Who in hell is going to spend money to dive on a bleached out dead reef? Enough about reefs for now, we will talk more about the reefs later." Carl said.

He completely switched the subject and started on us making changes to the house. "I was thinking about turning the dining room into our Game Room. The only thing that has ever been in that room is Brian's stereo. I have walked through that room for millions of years and could never think of anything I want to do with it. It's not like I do a lot of entertaining, I do not throw huge dinner parties; I could see no reason to do anything with it at all, beside I like eating in the kitchen."

"So, I was thinking we can turn the dining room into the Game Room. Sandra I will give you a great big bag full of money, the right year bills I might add. You and Brian zap up to 2017 and pick up two big desk top computers; a printer and you may as well get a lap top or two. Oh don't forget my Microwave oven."

"Sandra you talked me into letting you buy a big flat screen Television, so be it, but I am laying down a few ground rules. No TV in the kitchen that is my space.

You guys can hook up TV's in your bed rooms if you want and the big TV goes on the back wall in the living room. Can you live with that Sandra?"

"Carl I think that is more than fair, shake on it. They shook hands; Sandra said it is a done deal dude. Brian and I will take his truck and zap up to 2017, pick up everything and zap back and hook this stuff up. This is going to be so much fun." She grinned.

"While you two are doing that I am going to zap over to an office furniture store, pick up a huge desk and three top of the line leather office chairs and maybe a lamp or two, but first let's go for a swim."

It took us no time at all to toss in three air mats and dive into the pool along with Poe, man the 85 degree water feels unbelievable and of course the endless cooler was floating around with us. We floated on the mats; Poe was lying across Sandra's legs. Carl opened three Coors and handed one to Sandra and myself.

I took a long deep drink and thought to myself, man you are going shopping in 2017 for computers and a flat screen TV.

Dude you had never seen a computer till a little while ago and you have no idea in hell what a flat screen television even looks like. Man, I was sitting on the beach in 789 Hawaii less than thirty minutes ago dome time. Now I'm going shopping in the year 2017.

We finished the beers and it was time to get out of the pool, take a shower and get this project under way. As we walked toward the house, Carl and Sandra were talking. "I think I'm going to get on my lap top and check out what's available at Wal-Mart and Office Depot in the year 2017, then zap over and pick up the computers and televisions. I'm going to buy a ton of ink and printer paper. I am not into zapping to 2017 if we run out of ink. I love the idea of turning the dining room into the Game Room. The game is afoot to quote Sir Conan Doyle."

Sandra was kind of skipping as she spoke; "this is going to be so much fun."

Man I'm going to a Wal-Mart? I'm sure this is going to be a trip. I am going shopping 40 plus years in the future; this will be most entertaining no doubt about that I said to myself kind of shaking my head. *Why the hell not?*

It took me no time to shower and change, I walked into the kitchen and Sandra had her lap top open. It was sitting on the kitchen table, "come look at this Brian, it's the Wal-Mart web site; we can check out what they have in stock before we even go there."

Sure as hell I was looking at color photos of all these different brands of computers. It listed them by sizes, price and a new word I learned, giga bytes. Man we can pick out what we want before we walk into the store, this is amazing. She typed in flat screen TVs, and photos popped up. So that's what a flat screen TV looks like.

"Look what I just found Brian, what a fantastic big screen television, a 75 inch Samsung ultra HD smart LED, with curved glass screen. This will work great in the living room and it's only $6,500. I am going to take photos so I have all the stuff we want to buy on my phone and I can just show them what we want. Here is a great TV, for my room a 65 inch RCA less than $500, you want one Brian? She didn't wait for me to respond, look here are our desk tops, and we will get two of them. Apple 27 inch QHD 32 GB of ram, these are killer computers and they are only $2100 each. Okay we need a good printer and here is an OKI multifunction printer for only $550. Crap I forgot the lap tops, give me a second, she typed in lap top and said here it is, an Apple Macbook 12 inch intelcore 8 GB memory dude only $ 2000 each. And we can't forget Carl's microwave, here's a great 2.2 CU ft Panasonic for only $175. I think that about covers it."

"Brian, I got the photos in my phone we are ready." Man she was having a great time, she was grinning and her face was aglow.

"I hate to break your mood Sandra, but I just heard you throw out some pretty big price tags for all these items, Sandra, 17,000 or 18,000 thousand dollars is a lot of money. Carl won't be mad if you spend that much on electronic toys?" I asked her.

She looked at me and started to laugh so hard she could not speak. She started to say something and broke up again.

"Brian let me explain something about Carl, she was still kind of chuckling, he has no concept about money, and it means nothing to him. He is undoubtedly a billionaire many times over and does not know it, or even care. You see all those 5 gallon buckets he has stacked in the garage?" She asked me. I shook my head yes, there has to be 3 dozen of them just sitting there in nice neat stacks, I wondered what they were for Carl does not look like he is in to painting. "Brian 5 of those buckets are full of diamonds, 9 or 10 are filled with gold coins from all ages and places. For some reason he has one stuffed with confederate money, another couple are full of Roman coins. He has a bunch filled with raw gold from Sutter Mill. He has Jade and Rubies in buckets, all just sitting there. The man owns all the land around the Time Dome for miles. In his bed room are foot lockers filled with stocks and bonds."

"He has shoe boxes stuffed with cash from different years stacked up in his closet."

"Hell as you can tell by looking at the guy money has not gone to his head. Money is just part of time traveling to Carl, an inconvenience, so he made damn good and sure he would always have plenty of the shit around. He even calls it "that shit." The bag of money he handed me to go shopping has to have at least $35,000 in it and it's all in new $100 bills."

"Brian we are going to have so much fun, just wait till we pay these people with cash, they do freak. It is always a big to do; handing the cashier 170 brand new $100 bills is not done very often. But we are traveling at level 3 so they will not even remember it happened the next day."

"Sandra you know I never put any thought into to the fact Carl is rich; oh well if you got to have a roommate having a rich one helps."

"A point well taken" she added.

"Sandra I have to tell you straight up I have never been to a Wal-Mart before; I have heard of them but I have never been in one. I am not sure what to expect. I know it is some kind of a store, I gather it's a big place and they sell a variety of items."

"Damn it woman you have me going shopping. I never go shopping, I hate shopping. I even dread going to the supermarket but they sell beer and I do have to eat so I force myself deal with it. Sandra how the hell did you talk me into this?" She just smiled.

"Man I'm going up to the year 2017 for the third time in three days," I said shaking my head. She looked at me and smiled again.

Carl walked into the kitchen and poured a cup of coffee and lit the hash pipe. "Have you picked out what you want to get yet Sandra?"

Without waiting for a reply he said to me "Hey Brian this is your very first Wal-Mart adventure. Be warned; watch out for the fat women in black stretch pants," and he started to crack up, Sandra broke up too.

"Sandra poked me in the ribs, hey Brian give me a few minutes to put my hair up in rollers and we will be ready to go to Wal-Mart." This cracked them both up.

"Wait up guys you are both starting to freak me out, Disco was bad enough now you guys are dumping a Wal-Mart on me, not only a Wal-Mart but one 43 years in the future. Sometimes I think you guys just like fucking with me."

"He's wise to us Carl," Sandra said in a whisper.

They both cracked up.

"Carl I decided to zap to the Charlotte, North Carolina Wal-Mart. It's a super store, I checked it out and they have what I want in stock. I am going on a Tuesday early afternoon; I don't think Brian is ready for a Wal-Mart on a weekend yet. I'm heading down to the time pole to lock the number into my phone and we take off."

"We are going to go in Brian's Toyota; we will be back in a minute. This will be a ton of fun just watching Brian's face in a 2017 Wal-Mart, you sure you don't want to come Carl?"

"Na, said Carl I want to run out and pick out the office furniture. I will walk down with you and lock some numbers into my Zippo."

The two of them returned in no time, Sandra told Poe to stay and guard; he lay down and sighed looking at us with sad eyes. We walked out to our trucks; Carl said, "I made sure the tags on your truck are the right year, driving around in a 1970 Toyota pickup in 2017 will be noticed."

Carl got in his truck, waved, clicked his Zippo twice and was gone.

"I think you better let me drive Brian, I'm going to zap us in behind the store and we will drive around to the front. Never forget there are no rules in a Wal-Mart parking lot, she was laughing again. Are you ready for this dude?" she asked.

"No Sandra, I'm not ready for this."

She had her phone in her hand, she pushed a few buttons, I heard the wind sound and I was on my way to Charlotte N.C. in the year 2017 to go shopping for things I didn't even know existed till a little while ago.

"Say a few Syllables Moe!"
Chapter 24

I was looking at the back of a very long light gray cinder block building, it was not very tall maybe two stories, and we were sitting right across from a great big loading dock with sets of large retractable green doors. On Sandra's side of the truck was a line of parked truck trailers, on my side were a few big green dumpsters, behind them was a 10 foot high chain link fence that ran the length of the building. It was early afternoon and it was deserted, we saw nobody.

Out of no place came a loud voice. "Did you see that man? That truck came out of thin air, what the hell are we drinking?" I looked over and sitting on the curb leaning on the fence in the shade of the dumpster sat two pretty drunk homeless looking guys. "You have got to watch this Mad Dog 20/20 it plays tricks on you, that's why they call it Sneaky Pete," said the second bum. That is as far as it went with those two; it was the Sneaky Pete playing tricks on them.

"Brian, you are sitting 43 years in the future," Sandra said as she started the truck.

I waved and said, "Goodbye" to the bums. They waved and said goodbye back, nice guys.

This was one long- ass building, we got to the end and Sandra turned left; on the side of the building was a large automotive department with garages and the building was still going on.

We came to a stop sign and in front of me was a vast parking lot. Man we are talking 3 or 4 football fields of pavement, with these really tall light poles and lots of speed bumps. Abandoned shopping carts dotted the parking lot.

To my left was the front of the Wal-Mart it was damn near 1000 yards long, with doors on both ends and the middle. This place is fricking huge.

"Great said Sandra the place is pretty empty now, let's cut though the garden section, then we can walk through the store. Electronics is always in the back."

She parked the truck pretty close to the entrance; we got out and started to walk toward this monster of retail shopping. I felt like I was in a "Star Trek" rerun.

This place is overwhelming, there is stuff for sale on top of stuff for sale, and they have it divided into sections.

You want paint, it is in the paint section, you want Kids toys, you want a toaster, you want shoes, they all have their own areas, and hell they even sell food. Man this place is about every kind of store there is under one roof.

"Follow me Brian, let's get what we came for and get back to the dome. Brian you have a very intense look on your face," she said with a sound of concern in her voice.

"Sandra, I am going to have to think this whole trip over, but I'm with you let's get what we came for and get gone." "Good thinking Brian," quickly added Sandra.

"The electronics is right over there." She pointed and I followed. Sandra found someone who could help her. The woman working in electronics took one look at the list on Sandra's phone and called for two stock boys. As four of them started working on filling the list, I had time to wander around and take a better look at things.

I found out what a CD was, they looked kind of interesting. Holding a CD, I was amazed by the sheer amount of plastic of all types, kinds and forms.

Everywhere I looked I saw plastic. Just about everything was packaged in some kind of plastic.

Even the damn coat hangers are plastic. Carl had told us there has been a 600 % increase in the use of plastics since 1974 to 2017, but seeing it has a hell of lot more impact than hearing about it.

I was taken aback by how many of the various items in that store came from overseas, mostly from China. I checked labels and I could find almost nothing that said made in the U.S.A. I looked over and saw Sandra waving for me, I walked over and said. "What's up babe?"

"They filled my order and will load it into our truck off the loading dock out back, here is the fun part paying with cash. You got to see this."

"Will that be all Miss?" asked the cashier, Sandra nodded her head. The cashier pushed the total button and said "your total with tax and extended warranties comes to $18,380.53"

Sandra took her back pack off her shoulder, took out the rolled up paper bag and started to count out stacks of brand new $100 dollar bills.

The look on the cashiers face was one of shock.

"Are you paying with $19,000 in cash? She asked in a very shaky voice. I'm going have to call my manager."

It did not take him long to show up. He and Sandra spoke for a few minutes, they came to an understanding.

"Brian I am going to the office to pay for this, you can drive the truck around to the loading dock. I will be right out."

The two stock men had finished loading the stuff into the truck and tied it down, I tipped them $20 each, and they both looked very pleased. Just about then Sandra came walking out with the manager who was all smiles by her side. He shook her hand, and she smiled back. She got into the truck and said, "let's be gone Brian."

I drove back to the spot we landed; the two winos were still sitting there in the shade drinking Mad Dog 20/20. I decided to give them a thrill and let them watch us disappear. I pulled up next to them, and gave the horn a little honk, I leaned out the window and said, "See you guys later."

I flipped a crumbled up $10 bill out the window, and waved goodbye. They both said "Thanks Bro," and waved goodbye.

Sandra pushed the button on her cell phone, I heard the wind sound and the truck was back in the dome's garage filled with new toys.

Carl's truck was all ready in the garage with six or seven boxes in the bed; a few of the boxes were pretty big. He was not to be found, we walked through the house and out to the front porch, he was sitting there rocking in his chair drinking a Coors, with Poe sleeping next to him. As soon as the dog heard Sandra he ran right over to her, with his tail going a zillion miles an hour. She sat down petting him. Telling him he was a good boy and Poe settled right down. Damn that dog loves Sandra, no two ways about that.

"Hey guys did you get all the stuff" Carl asked. Sandra said, "Yes we did Carl, and I have some money left over."

"Don't worry about that Sandra, just hang on to it and you use it for whatever. It's of no matter." He said.

Sandra is right; money means nothing to Carl, but that is not a bad place to be I thought to myself.

Carl went on, "I got some real nice things guys, wait 'till you see the chairs I got and the desk is twelve feet long. Now we have to unload everything and put it together and hook it all up, but first we smoke some hash and drink a few Coors, getting all this together is going to take the rest of the day."

"In the background I could hear the Stones playing the song "Under my Thumb." Man those guys can rock. I do love our sound system.

After about 10 minutes Sandra said, "let's get to it boys it will not get done by itself." We got up and started unpacking various items out of their boxes, putting things together and hooking them up.

Carl was right, it took hours to unpack everything and put it all together. I must admit the frequent hash breaks added a bit of time to the project. At long last we stood there looking at our handy work; there is now a big screen TV hanging on the living room wall, and we have our own real live office.

The empty dining room had been transformed into our "Game Room" the desk looked great, the two desk top computers and printer fit on it perfect, we even had two nice bright lamps, the leather chairs felt so comfortable and it was fun to spin around in them.

Sandra spoke up, "I don't know about you guys but I'm going for a swim and I'm getting hungry".

"Yeah I'm into getting wet myself and then I will whip us up some dinner, Carl said.

Tonight is pot luck or I can zap out and get us some fish sandwiches."

"Fish sandwiches Carl?" Sandra stated to laugh; Carl and I had to join her. It had been a long day and we had got a lot done.

"I am into a fast swim, grab some dinner and go to bed early and get a fresh start tomorrow. Besides Brian we can try out the new TV in my bed room." Sandra suggested.

"Sandra I'm not too sure about this TV in the bed room thing. I can think of better ways of spending our time in bed besides watching television." She smiled and poked me in my ribs.

"Good thinking an early start on a fresh day is a great idea, Sandra. Let's get wet, dig up some food and hit the hay early. What do ya think?" asked Carl

We all got up and started walking to the pool; Sandra had Poe right by her side.

Damn today has been one more very strange day, I had been surfing in Hawaii in the year 789, then I went to a Wal-Mart in 2017, where Sandra spent almost twenty thousand dollars on a pile of electronic gizmos. We are now hooked up to the Twenty First Century and all this took place in one day.

Save that Thought
Chapter 25

I woke up in Sandra's bed, and I looked at the clock, it was 7:00 a.m. Sandra was up and gone. I knew she would be up early and playing with her new toys. Against the far wall was her new big screen TV. We had watched a bit of television last night. She knew a lot of the programs and filled me in as she went along. The picture was clear and sharp and I fell in love with the remote control. Man I could change the channel, raise and lower the volume all with my thumb. I'm sure I made Sandra crazy with my remote control antics. The TV I left in the old house was a square box, it had a black and white picture, with rabbit ears and tin foil hanging on them. I had to get up to change the channels and on a good day I could kind of get five stations, maybe. Being zapped into the futures has certain advantages.

I decided I should get my day started and catch up with Sandra and Carl. It took no time to get myself together and walk out to the Game Room.

They both looked up from the computer and said "Good morning Brian", at the same time. Then they turned and looked back at whatever they were doing. It looked like they were into something on the computer as they sat drinking coffee, and chatting.

Carl turned and said, "Brian I was waiting for you before I whipped up some breakfast, Sandra and I decided to try and get a grip on our new toys. You are going to have so much fun playing with these computers. Come on in the kitchen and grab a cup of coffee, I will cook up some chow."

Sandra got up and said "I need to stretch." She stuck her arms way up in the air, stood on her toes and with a flick of her hair she took a deep breath.

I like the way that girl stretches, I had to grin. We poured some coffee and sat at the table as Carl started to make breakfast.

"French toast, bacon ok?" He asked. "Sounds great, Carl I love the smell of bacon frying." Sandra replied.

"Light a bowl of hash Brian and by the way what did you think about the 2017 Wal-Mart adventure?" he asked me.

"Carl, I been giving this a lot of thought, overwhelming is the first impression. There are more items for sale than I could comprehend. It is meant for people to fill their carts with anything they can possibly want or think they need. The whole building is set up so you cannot buy one thing. It is retail gone insane, stuffed under one roof.

The second thing I noticed was the place was awash in plastics, every where there is plastic. Buy dish washing soap it's in plastic, laundry soap; bleach all come in plastic jugs that get tossed out. Man you buy vegetables and you stick them in a plastic bag that goes into a bigger plastic bag. A person can buy a case of water and it comes in little plastic bottles wrapped in plastic.

Used once, tossed away and in a few days that person can buy some more water and repeat the process. Man you can buy disposable plastic razors that come in a plastic bag, just throw the razor out when it get dull, is not life wonderful?"

"Are you guys following my drift here? I asked. These are the observations of a person from forty years in the past, yanked up and dropped into the middle of a 2017 retail monster. The sheer amount of plastic is an eye opener."

"Something else I noticed was that almost nothing was made in America; I checked dozens of labels, lots of stuff made overseas and it was being sold at a pretty low price."

"I had to wonder what happens to small town stores when a giant like this opens and can sell an item for less than the small business operation pays for the same thing. You asked and I told you" I concluded.

Sandra looked at me and said, "Brian seeing the world though a different pair of eyes can make a person take a fresh look at things they have become accustomed to seeing. I have grown up shopping in one Wal-Mart or another. It has come to the point I no longer notice the things you observed for the first time today."

"There is a hollow feeling in my chest when I realize the amount of plastic that has been introduced into our world in the last 40 years. Most of all what shocks me is people have become numb to the fact plastic is swallowing us alive." I said.

"Breakfast is almost done will you guys be kind enough to set the table?" Carl asked. "With the time zapped clean plates and silver ware Carl?" Sandra was laughing again and I do love the sound of that laugh. "Hey Sandra time zapping dishes clean works, it's easy, and besides I don't own any dish washing soap." Breakfast was super; I ate my fill and then some. Sandra spoke up as she took a bite of French toast, "I'm glad the Dorian effect will not let us get fat." We sat at the table drinking coffee and smoking hash, it was quiet and cool.

"Well Guys, Carl asked, what do you want to do next? We can go to the game room and start laying out our plan to save the world or we can go surfing."

Carl had a huge grin on his face; "we can put it to a vote. I vote surfing."

"Me too I said. I vote surfing."

"Poe and I vote we stay here and start on our plan so that makes it a tie and as you know in the event of a tie Sandra wins."

"Hell, I didn't even know Poe could vote Carl questioned and I don't remember that tie rule do you Brian? I think she made it up."

No matter, whatever Carl and I said we were going to the game room to begin laying out the plan to save the world. The Game room was big; the long desk fit well next to the wall, Carl had picked up a stand for the stereo, so it was off the floor now. Even with the two desk top computers, the printer and the lamps, there was still a lot of space left. Sandra had purchased a stack of notebooks and pens she had placed on the side of the desk.

"Sandra began to lay out her plan. "Here's the way I see it we have two computers, one will be the Game computer and the other will be our personal home computer. We cannot continue to ditty bop through time without sooner or later running into ourselves. As we know that would never do. So we need to start keeping a record of dates, places and times we travel to. Besides I'm sure it will be most interesting reading. I like doing stuff like that so I will be happy to keep up on it besides, it will be fun. The adventures of 3 Time Travelers put down in writing, kind of like our journal."

"Okay it is settled. The computer on the left will be our play with computer. The one on the right is for nothing but the Game. Is that okay with you guys?" She asked.

Sandra was good at putting Carl and I in a spot where there was only one answer and she already knew what it would be before she asked the question. We both said "Okay Sandra."

"Plan "A" is for us to write down what we think are the most important issues. Then categorize them, and then we do the research on each one and decide what is the best way to deal with them one at a time. Some of the problems will be smaller and easier to deal with. Others will take a great deal of effort to get into motion. We may be forced to attempt changes in more than one problem area at a time. We have to set realistic goals for ourselves as well as some kind of time line we can attempt to follow."

"Sounds like you have been putting a good deal of thought into this Sandra" Carl looked at her; I like your plan girl. Now can we go surfing?"

"Carl you are hopeless and I know you had all the time in the world to become hopeless." She replied.

"Tell you what Carl, let's get started on the list and then we will go surfing, this won't take long and it would make me happy." I knew Carl would give in to Sandra.

"Okay Sandra, let's get started listing the major problems. Carl sat down, he opened a pad, grabbed a pen and said its show time boys' and girls'."

"Global warming is on the top of the list, and there is going to be a zillion sub topics listed under that one heading. Plastic is the second big issue once again a zillion sub topics. Pollution, of the air, water and ground is next on the list. Nukes should be added to the list. That one is going to be a back breaker. These four are the biggest problems I can see, I'm sure we will run across others along the way but let's start with these. You are right Carl I have been doing a lot of thinking about this.

She looked at us and said "I hope we are up for it."

"We will take every one of these problems and do as much research as we can and look for places we can make changes. The first challenge is education of the public and the second part of that is teaching children about recycling and the dangers of global warming starting at a very early age, Sandra went on, people can be changed."

"Look you two; remember back before I was born when everyone smoked cigarettes. Hell that's right Brian 1974 is still in the middle of the smoking epidemic, by the year I was living in 2016 smoking is very restricted and almost nobody smokes by then."

"Sandra back when I was a kid, smoking was cool and hip; you could not turn on TV without a commercial for cigarettes. They pounded it into you, it was everywhere you looked, news papers, bill boards, and magazines.

In the 1950's Television programs were sponsored by different brand of cigarettes. They even had jingles people walked around singing. Smoking made you a man, smoking was sexy for women. Hell Humphrey Bogart was famous for his style of smoking. It was part of our culture.

Smoking was allowed on airplanes, in city buses, in restaurants and bars, or just walking down the street, it was an accepted part of everyday life. You had a cup of coffee and a smoke. When I grew up smoking was everywhere. Every old black and white movie and rerun TV program I have ever seen had people smoking in it. Surfing is the only thing that kept me from starting to smoke."

"It's not like that anymore Brian, stores now have cigarettes locked up, and the cost of a pack is about $5 or more. Now less than 40 years later you almost never see anyone smoking. It took changes in the laws, it took changes in peoples opinion of smoking, it took extensive education of the public to bring about these changes, but it worked and it can work again, starting with plastics."

"Don't get me wrong there are still people who smoke, but it is not like it once was. You guys see where I'm going with this? She asked. If the tobacco industry can be brought into line why not the plastic manufacturers?"

Carl spoke up, "Hey you two don't be looking at me because I smoke. I do not smoke that much. Besides I only smoke cigarettes to keep my Zippo lighter "Bob" happy, he enjoys lighting cigarettes." Carl added "I like that lighter." He had that grin on his face again.

We both looked at him. He said before that he only smokes to keep his lighter happy. We looked at each other and shook our heads. "Whatever Carl," Sandra said grinning.

I have to admit Sandra is one very smart woman and she was right about educating the public, but how? The public can be changed; we know that for a fact. It is still a matter of how we can get this into motion.

"Okay Sandra we have four of the major problems listed. The research and outlining our plan of action is next. I think that this is a very logical way to go about introducing changes. Now can we go surfing Sandra?" He poked her shoulder.

"Carl you are such a little kid, yeah we can go surfing now said Sandra, but when we get back we get started with our research, promise Carl?"

"Yes I promise Sandra."

Man I could not help but thinking, I'm going surfing and then I'm coming home and start saving the world. I have never saved the world before. I have not a clue how one goes about saving a world, but that's okay, I love making things up as I go along.

Name that Tune.
Chapter 26

"Cool we are going surfing; I want to go back to Queens. My surfing improved a lot surfing there and I get to pick the time and date. Said Carl, he was one big grin. I want to go back to 8:08 a.m. on August 8 th in the year 808.

Got it? 808808808 is that not one cool date?" We look at Carl. He looked very pleased with himself.

Sandra and I looked at each other, She said, "Looks like we are going surfing in Hawaii in the year 808, Why the hell not?"

"Think that one up by yourself did ya Carl?" Sandra asked laughing.

"Hey Sandra that is one cool date" I said coming to Carl's defense. Besides I like surfing Queens and since it is helping Carl's surfing improve, I'm all for it."

"Okay with me guys, but this is going to be a quick trip, an hour or so. We will leave Poe here; after all we will only be got one minute dome time. Let's bring nothing but our boards and paddle right out."

"No endless cooler Sandra, no lawn chairs, no hash? Carl said "No Carl, we are going there to surf, you can bring the hash if it makes you happy," she gave in.

"The endless cooler hates it when he has to stay home. He has become used to following me around. I really think I hurt its feeling when I do not bring him along." Carl sounded so sincere as he said this.

Sandra and I once again look at each other; this statement is definitely one of Carl's strangest. But we are talking about a guy who smokes cigarettes to keep his time traveling Zippo lighter he named "Bob" happy and does not wash dishes, he time zaps then back to a point they are clean. Not too much out of Carl's mouth takes us by surprise any more, but this had us both shaking our heads. The beer cooler will be sad if we leave it home? We could only look at each other and grin.

Sandra spoke up "Carl we are going surfing, the only thing we need to take with us is our boards and a bar of surf wax, trust me on this one, I have gone surfing more than a few times, I know how the game is played. I'm sure the cooler will get over it if we leave it home."

"Okay Sandra, the endless cooler stays home this trip; I just hate to hurt its feelings," Carl relented.

"Hurting the coolers feelings? My God you are such a mess Carl. I know what you are going to say Carl, that you have had all the time in the world to become a mess. Sandra continued, Can you believe this guy Brian? I never know if he is putting us on or not."

"What's to believe Sandra? We live with Carl the first, keeper of time, the universe and all things, nothing he does or says surprises me anymore. So let's surfing."

It took us no time to get changed, grab our boards and meet up at the time pole. Of course the endless cooler was sitting by Carl's chair. He looked up the number dialed about 25 numbers on the old phone held his Zippo by the phone hung up and said "I got it."

Sandra told Poe to "stay and guard the time dome", he looked at her as if to say "yeah sure thing", he lay down on the grass on his back rolled around a few times and went to sleep.

Carl leaned over petted the cooler and said "you stay home and be a good boy, I will be right back". I swear I could hear the cooler whimper a little.

"Okay let's go surfing now everyone is learning how, next stop Hawaii in the year 808."

He clicked his lighter twice, Sandra and I pushed the buttons on our time travel watches. We heard the wind sound and we were standing in the rain on Waikiki beach.

"It's raining boys and girls I said, but the rain is 76 degrees the air is 76 degrees, and the water is 76 degrees.

The surf is 4 foot and totally glassy, I see no problems here. I'm paddling out," and I started walking toward the water.

"Let me stash our bag and I will be right out." She stuck the bag under a few palm leaves and joined us.

This is unbelievable, the ocean feels great; I am going surfing in a Hawaiian rain storm and I am heading out into beautiful waves.

"I am going to paddle out with you guys and try catching some waves on the outside break." Said Carl.

He was doing very good keeping up with Sandra and me; he got out to the lineup no problem.

Sandra was sitting up on her board and looking outside. "Here comes your wave Carl, get ready and paddle when I tell you to. Wait, wait, okay now paddle dude."

Damn if he didn't catch his first real wave, he got the board to turn right and ride the face of the wave a pretty far ways and even managed kind of a kick out. Sandra and I were both yelling as loud as we could. He paddled back out looked at us and said "I want to do that again." he said with a huge grin.

"Carl you are going to be hell to live with from now on," Sandra, said as she splashed him.

We traded waves, Carl did very well, he was still pulling some dumb beginner mistakes but he got a lot of very nice rides.

Surfing in the rain was magic, it was a soul cleaning rain, and it was what we needed. No thoughts, we just allowed ourselves to drift off and be one with nature.

Once again time passed way too fast. "We should be heading back to the dome. We have been surfing for almost two hours, let me get my bag and we will head back. You did great Carl." Sandra said.

We caught a wave in; standing on the beach the rain felt unbelevieable, we just stood there letting the rain wash the salt water off our bodies. Sandra grabbed her bag and took Carl's Zippo out of the bag and handed it to him, "Let's go home Carl." She said.

He clicked the Zippo six times; we heard the wind sound and were standing in the North Carolina sun right by the time pole. Poe was still sleeping in the grass and the endless cooler looked no worse for being left alone.

As soon as Poe heard Sandra he was right up next to her, his tail wagging like the wind.

"That was a ton of fun surfing in the rain, you guys want a Coors?" Carl leaned over, patted the cooler and said "Good boy," reached in and gabbed 3 cans. He opened them and we sat back in our lawn chairs, drinking ice cold Coors and drying in the warm North Carolina sun, just enjoying being alive.

Sandra spoke, "Let go for a fast swim, and get changed, get settled in and then get started working on the list."

"You know Sandra we are opening a Pandora's Box and we have no idea where it will take us. Carl said, but I promised you Sandra, so let's get started. By the way surfing was a lot of fun, the rain was amazing. I feel like I'm ready to start on playing the game now."

Once again I can only shake my head, I had just been surfing the rain in Hawaii in the year 808, now it is time to go for a swim and then we get started on saving the world.

I think the word boring is no longer in my vocabulary.

"That's all Folks"
Chapter 27

I could hear the Television as I walked into the Game room; Sandra was sitting on the new couch in the living room she had our new flat screen on the local news. "I wanted to check out the new flat screen T.V., I just love this picture, is this not fantastic Brian?"

"I have to admit it is a very life like picture, the colors are so clean, the sound is like being in a movie theater, this thing is unbelievable, once more I am welcomed to the future." I said back to Sandra.

Carl walked in and sat down on the far end of couch and put his feet up on the Tucson sign. "Wow that is a beautiful picture Sandra, you did good woman. If we have to have television we may as well have the top of the line."

"There, that is an example of the Death floaters." said Carl in a loud voice as he pointed toward the Flat screen.

I had not been paying any attention to what was on the TV set, turns out it was the local new broadcast, and they just covered a story about a man killing his wife, her mother and a few other people and then he shot himself and committed suicide.

"Death Floaters?" I asked.

"That is classic death floater; you see they feed off death and fear. They take over a body; use it to kill other people so they can feed off their deaths and their fear. Often times it is mindless killings, they generate more fear. Death and fear is what they live off. In order for them to move to the next host, the person who did the killing must kill themselves or the death floater is stuck in that body and will die when that body dies. It has to end with suicide for the death floater to leave the killers body."

"The larger the number of deaths and the more horrific the deaths are the longer the death floater can rest between meals. There are only a few thousand of them in the world; luckily they only breed if there has been a major killing. They don't really breed; they divide into another death floater who then goes on its merry way.

"Jones Town stuffed a bunch of them for a long time and produces a new generation of death floaters. Columbine in 1999 is a classic example of the death floaters having a meal and reproducing."

"What is Columbine Carl and what is Jonestown?" I asked.

"Sorry Brian I keep forgetting you are living in 1974. Columbine is the name of a high school in Colorado; in 1999 two students went on a killing spree in that school. They shot and killed 13 people and then killed themselves."

"Jonestown will be founded in a few years in Guyana, by a religious group of over 900 people under the Guidance of some dude named Jim Jones. Anyway in November 1978 Jones forces his followers to drink poison cool aid and then kills himself. That is classic death floater, murder, fear and suicide. Killing and suicide has been going on for as long as I can remember, death floaters have been around a long time and what is really freaky is these events are happening more often.

Death floaters are a very strange life form, but they are a living thing, none the less, in order to live they must feed. I don't even think there is anyone besides me who knows they exist, but they are out there, you hear about them all the time, and now you two know what you are hearing.

Don't get me wrong murder is still just murder, but if it ends with the killer committing suicide, chances are it's a death floater having a snack."

"Death floaters", Sandra and I said at the same time, looking at Carl's face.

"Yep, death floaters." He had a huge grin.

Damn we never know if Carl is putting us on or not.

All Sandra and I could do was look at each other with our mouths open; living with Carl will constantly get your attention.

Just like that Carl changed the subject and stated talking about the flat screen TV again. "I love the picture on that flat screen Sandra, like I said you did good woman. That is a great TV, said Carl. Hey Sandra can you get MTV on that TV?" He asked.

"Sure thing Carl it's hooked up to the time pole, we can get any year you want. I think the early 80's had the best videos. You got to remember I was not born till 1989, so I'm going off what I have been told," she said as she started playing with the remote control. Next thing I know I was looking at a long haired glam rock band rocking out at full volume, the lead singer jumped up and kicking the air right there in front of my face on this huge screen.

"Go ahead and jump" were the first words I heard come out of MTV. So that's MTV, I said to myself, I could get to like this. "Great picture Sandra, Carl repeated. Turn it down some and let's get started with the Game." We all slowly got up and headed toward the Game room.

Sandra asked, "You guys want something to drink?" Carl and I both said "Dr. Pepper, please."

Carl and I walked into the game room and took a seat in front of the game computer. I love how comfortable the big leather chairs are; I just had to spin around once, well maybe twice.

Sandra came in holding three bottles of Dr. Pepper, handed one to Carl and me and said "Use the coasters boys." My God Sandra has turned into "June Cleaver," I thought to myself, I am living in a re run of Leave it to Beaver and started to laugh. "So coasters are funny Brian?" Sandra had that look in her eyes. "Na babe coasters are fine." I smiled at her. She sat in the middle chair and pulled up to the desk and started to type.

"Let's pick a subject that is fresh in our minds, let's look up the great northern garbage patch and see if we can get a realistic idea of what it will take to clean it up and if indeed it can be cleaned up at all. We will see where that takes us and then we follow the Yellow brick road. Sandra added. I'm sure this will be a can of worms."

"Well this is cheerful news; according to this we cannot clean the mess up. This dude is taking about it will take 70 boats dragging football field size nets working 10 hours a day one year to clean up 1% of the Northern pacific garbage patch and that's just the garbage they can net. A lot of the waste matter will slip right through the nets. Only 1% of the northern ocean cleaned in one year for the cost of $500 million plus a year.

Man that is looking at 100 years of work and still not getting all the mess. Prevention is brought up as the solution. Once again stopping the mess before it gets in the water is the key."

"What you are saying Sandra is the plastic that is out there is going to remain out there. Cleaning up of the mess is too costly and time consuming and will not be 100 % effective, correct?" I asked her. "Roger" she replied.

"Guys she went on, we have a lot more research to do, this is the first study about a cleanup I came across, and it's pretty old, let's see if there is a light at the end of the tunnel."

"I think we should move up a few years and see what 2018 has to say about the clean up. Things change; this will take no time" and she started typing.

"This shows promise, there is a Dutch company named

"The Ocean Cleanup" who came up with a new device that is a mile long made up of 40 foot long air filled plastic tubes that floats on the surface dragging a net 10 feet deep under the booms. It will be weighted and shaped like a big "U." They are going to begin tests in San Francisco in the summer of 2018. If it works it will clean up half the Garbage patch in 5 years. They are talking about deploying 60 of these things and just let them float around pushed by currents picking up plastic. They just have to be cleaned out every few weeks, and it will not collect the microplastics that are too small to be caught in the netting. Wow is this a light at the end of the tunnel?"

Sandra kept reading. "There are a few questions, like will the nets trap and kill sea life, like fish, turtles, etc.

The Dutch are saying the nets are not that deep and that sea life can swim under them. Turns out these things are going to have to be towed out to the Garbage patch that will take time, and make it just about impossible to relocate them in case of storms. However the counter is these long floating booms are strong enough to with stand severe storms."

"Sandra, I have spent a good deal of time in storms at sea. I have been on the ships wheel, and seen the bow of a 600 foot ship go under a wave that washed over the deck and containers. The surge of water hits the ships house with such force that the water went up 4 stories high and over the bridge wing. The whole ship shudders. I have been in storms that pound the ship for days. We are talking days and nights without stop you can hear and feel the impact of the ocean as it hits the ship. Storms so bad that you moved your mattress onto the deck in your cabin so you don't get knocked out of your bunk. The Storm at sea is the most powerful force of nature I have ever encountered. Storms at sea just don't care; they break, bend, twist and sink things that get in their way. It is nothing personal, it is a storm and that's what they are supposed to do. Been there, done that and I am telling you, that's the way it is. I added. These floating boom things are going to have to be super strong to withstand the power of a pissed off ocean."

"Brian you worked on the merchant ships you have seen the power of the ocean first hand and have a better understanding of it then I ever will, but I'm looking for a ray of light. Just the fact someone is attempting to do something is hopeful." Sandra had a big grin on her face.

"Let's take a break, go out on the pouch, drink a few Coors and talk about this. For the first time since the Game started we came up with some good news, I feel pretty positive about that. I can't help but think maybe the situation is not so hopeless after all. Sandra went on; in the last few days we have been slapped in the face with so much ugliness. Just knowing there are people who are trying to make changes is encouraging. Yeah this is a good place to take a break and take a deep breath."

A Silver Lining
Chapter 28

The porch was cool and quite, we have become fond of sticking our feet up on the rail and chilling out.

"You guys want a Coors?" As always the endless cooler was sitting next to Carl, he reached in grabbed three cans of Coors opened them and handed one to Sandra and I.

"Well I don't know about you two but finding out there are other people who are aware of these problems and are attempting to correct them is great news to me," Sandra said as she took a long drink of Coors.

Sandra continued, "So far I have read of a few places that say keeping the plastic out of the water is the only way to get a grip on the situation. You cannot clean up the mess if it is being added to daily. That has different parts to it; education of the public keeps coming up. Laying these floating collector booms across access points into the ocean is a suggestion. However the number one issue is to get the plastic industry to change its packaging. More or less stop making single use plastics, producing only recyclable plastics. There has to be some kind of a plastic tax to raise money to clean up what is out there. Clean up is not just dumping the crap into a land fill but sorting it out and disposing of it in a less harmful manner."

She continued "There is a lot involved in this clean up thing. They need to put into place worldwide Recycling centers. Not just a dumping ground, but locations the plastic is sorted and recycled if possible; if it cannot be recycled it must be disposed of in an orderly manner."

"There has to be some way of compressing the plastic into small blocks, like they do to junk cars and stored till it can be disposed of in a safe clean manner. But most of all, she said it comes down to stop making single use plastics."

"They cannot throw plastic in with things like food waste and paper and cardboard and wood, stuff that will break down and decompose in time. Landfills could become giant compost piles; and produce useful top soil that can be used in farming. Landfills cannot continue to be the collect all garbage pits they are being used for today. Bury it and forget it has to go. They have to get out of using land fill as a dumping ground." What do ya think she asked?

"Sandra what you are saying makes nothing but sense. In a perfect world it would work great. Just having this conversation is proof the world is far from perfect. Sandra we are dealing with countries where the average income is less them $600 a year. Countries where twelve year old boys walk around with AK 47's.

Places with way too many people, places where the sheer number of people overwhelm the infrastructure if there is any infrastructure to begin with. We are talking about parts of the world where a total of up to 10,000 people die a day due to water born diseases. Problem is these are the biggest polluting nations. Some of the poorest nations are also doing lots of the damage to the world, on land in the air and the water, but let's just deal with cleaning up plastic. Maybe you are right Sandra putting a value on all plastic would be enough incentive to get the poor nations to clean up what plastic is out there. This is the plastic clean up industry at its lowest level, people picking up useless trash and turning it into money. Something is always better than nothing," Carl concluded.

We could hear the Stones talking in the background.

The song "Around and Around" started to play.

"Joint was rocking, going around and around, what a crazy sound." We sat sipping Coors with our feet up on the rail, just watching the clouds blow by in the early fall winds.

"Man it is such a nice day I think I will open the dome up, and let the wind blow through. That's right; neither of you two has ever been here when I opened up the dome."

"Carl you can open the dome up?" asked Sandra.

"Well not the whole dome, but I can make four sides slide part way open. I do it on nice days and to air the place out. Sometimes In the winter I like to open it up and let the cold in, that's why I have woodstoves in every room. I even open it up in the rain. The Time Pole, the phone and the table always stay dry, not sure why but I have never seen them or the lawn chairs get wet. It's like they have some kind of shield around them."

"The dome is a pretty damn big place, when I open the sides the wind blows right through, it's fun to do. I like to open it up when it snows; it's really fun letting the snow in. Yeah, said Carl I will open the dome up for us right now."

Carl got up and said "Come on you guys I will show you how this works." We all got up and started walking toward the time pole and of course Poe was right next to Sandra.

As we were on our way to the pole Carl said, "Remind me to have a chat with the Ziplinks about us now having a dog." He went on "The Ziplinks come in the dome every few weeks and eat the grass, to keep it from growing out of control. They just take a few inches off the top. The grass looks great when they finish. Eating the grass is like a big event for them. I'm not sure but I think it's like a giant Ziplinks tail gate party. Maybe even a religious event or a Ziplinks Woodstock."

"Or perhaps all three rolled into one big happening, I'm not sure. Anyway it is a huge party for them, they can get pretty rowdy, and I try to be gone when they are munching down the grass."

"I think they get a buzz eating the grass; those Ziplinks can get pretty crazy. Millions of stoned out Ziplinks blasting out really loud music. Ziplinks music is kind of a high pitched buzzing, it sounds like a room full of 1000's of pissed off bumble bees at 78 rpm. Their music drives me up the wall, so I make a point to take a trip when they show up; some of these parties last a few days." Carl was cracking up as he spoke.

"Anyway the Ziplinks throw these huge grass eating parties and they look to be having lots of fun and I get the grass cut for free, so it is a good deal all the way around.

Now we have Poe and he is peeing and pooping on the grass, I'm not sure how that will sit with the Ziplinks, a pile of dog crap sitting in the middle of their feast."

Once again Sandra and I looked at each other, we never know if Carl is putting us on or not. The Ziplinks get high eating the grass in the Time

Dome? Dog crap ruining the Ziplinks feast? That sounds so weird, but it fits in with everything else in our lives.

"I am definitely going to have a talk with the Ziplinks high council about Poe. Carl went on, with the translator ring we can talk to them, after all they are our neighbors. I want to stay on good terms with them, last thing we need is 50 million Ziplinks pissed off at us over dog shit."

Sandra and I were still looking at each other shaking our heads. *Why the hell not?*

Carl picked up the Time Travel phone and dialed the number 220 and hung up. We heard a sound like someone opening sliding glass doors and could immediately feel the early fall breeze start to blow through the dome. I could smell the pines; the breeze was cool and felt so refreshing. The Time Dome truly is an amazing place.

We sat in our lawn chairs and of course the endless cooler was right by Carl's chair. "You guys ready for a fresh Coors? How about a bowl of hash? He asked.

I am glad we found some good news about people trying to clean up the plastics in the oceans. Let sit here a little while and chill and then head back to the game room and see what we come up with next okay? Sandra asked with a bit of a grin. Carl, pass me a beer and light up the pipe, we still have lots of work facing us." She added.

"Okay with me guys." I said.

Man I was still trying to get around the fact Ziplinks get high eating our lawn, and have rock out parties in the time dome.

Damn my life gets stranger every day. I could hear the Stones playing "Time is on my side" in the background.

Man, I love Time Travel.

Well that covers that!
Chapter 29

The fall wind was from the north about 10 miles an hour, just enough to cool everything down. The dome is so quiet when the Stones are not recording, it is haunting. The damn quite almost hurts your ears. Just the wind in the trees and now and then the song of a bird.

"Man it is beautiful here said Sandra, I could sit here all day and do nothing and not feel the least bit guilty about it. But we have a game to play, so let's get cracking."

She stood up and stretched again, I could spend hour's just watching Sandra stretch.

"You are right Sandra let get back to playing the game said Carl, Brian are you coming?"

I replied "sure thing, I will be right there". I was so comfortable sitting back, soaking up the beauty of a bright cool North Carolina morning, I did not feel like moving, but I really did not have much choice in the matter.

"Damn" I said to myself, I guess it is time to play the Game again as I slowly got up and started walking towards the house. I was in no rush to jump back into this mess. Until a few days ago, I had no idea any of this crap was going on. Ten days ago I was sitting in 1974 minding my own business and now I am playing a game to save the world from itself. Any thought of me saving the world had never crossed my mind before now, but then again I never had any thoughts of me riding in a hydrogen bomb blast for fun and I did that a few days ago.

Brian, face the facts you have no idea what is going to happen next in your life. Your wildest imagination cannot come close to whatever is really going to happen next. You are bouncing around in time like a pinball. Right now you are going up to play a huge game of save the world.

Why do I feel like I should be wearing a cape and have theme music playing in the background? Disguised as a mild mannered surfer, our hero is able to save the world with his bare hands, etc, etc.etc. All I could do was shake my head.

Carl, Sandra and Poe had a pretty long head start on me and were sitting at the computer as I walked in. I sat down next to Sandra.

"We left the computer on 2018, plastic clean up. Let's see where that takes us. She started typing; she shook her head and started to type again, and said this is more like it. The UN has started a global campaign to eliminate single use plastics by the year 2022. That's encouraging.

They named it the "Clean Seas Campaign". Basically they are saying plastic has gone too far and the problem needs to be addressed on a global level. These are the same issues we brought up, start cleaning up the mess and stop making single use plastic. The U N just started Clean Seas up in 2017 and have 50 countries signed up, and those countries account for over half the world coast lines. And some of those countries are among the world's poorest nations. I like reading good news" said Sandra.

"I hate playing Loki, but the facts are pretty damn scary said Carl. The equivalent of one garbage truck a minute is being dumped into the oceans every day. That adds up to millions of tons of crap a year that ends up floating in the ocean."

"Carl you are right, that's what is going on right now as we speak, but the U N is talking about precisely what we brought up earlier.

Number one, stop producing single use plastic worldwide.

Number two, educate the public to change their throw away life style, and to stop using single use plastics.

Number three, start cleaning up all the plastic that is already out there. We are talking cleaning up plastic both on land and in the oceans.

"In order for this to work it has to become a worldwide law, with a tax on all plastics."

Sandra continued. "The oceans make up over 70% of the surface of the earth and they are quickly becoming a populated waste land. We are getting very close to irreversible damage being done to all the oceans and seas. Micro plastics are floating in every ocean in the world; they are being eaten by fish, plastic is in the food chain. Micro plastics are killing off tremendous numbers of fish. This report spells it out, if we continue to dump plastics carelessly at the current rate by 2050 there will be more plastic in the oceans than fish. Damn we are back into the glum shit again," said Sandra.

"Okay the way I see it cleaning up the plastic mess is a way to start turning poverty around. A value on all plastics would have it cleaned up in no time, both on land and in the water near the coast. Dealing with the clean up in an orderly manner could produce a long term recycling industry. There has to be a worldwide plastic tax to make this work."

Carl shook his head and went on "We have got to stop plastic from getting into the water to begin with, and we have to get as much of that crap out of the oceans as soon as we can."

"I am not done yet, he grinned, in the last 45 years between plastic, global warming and overfishing, fish of all types and species all over the world are dying out. Dude we are talking about becoming extinct, like gone forever. Countless people throughout the world depend on fishing to eat. A healthy fish population is a must.

Worldwide, fish is the staple of the everyday diet. A healthy fish population cannot be maintained if poison is constantly being dumped into the oceans."

"Fishing is a multibillion dollar industry, that employs God knows how many people worldwide and feeds billions. A collapse of fishing would be the collapse of the world as we know it. Everyone in the whole fucking world has to be made aware that plastic is real, it is killing our oceans and it is happening right now."

Carl took a deep breath. "Now the big question how do we go about doing such a thing?"

"I got it!" Sandra exclaimed in a bold voice. She stood up, walked a few feet away, turned and looked at Carl then at me, "Let's write a book." Her green eyes sparkled.

Carl and I looked at each other in silence for a few seconds, "Write a book Sandra?" Carl asked.

"Sure guys it will work, we can write about all the things we have seen firsthand and tell the world about global warming, oceans full of plastic, wild fires running rampant, dead zones, reefs dying and poisoned water. We can spell it out for them."

"Hey world read this book and get the crap scared out of you. Now, get off your ass and go out and do something about it."

"Sandra we have a bit of a problem, nobody in the world knows anything about time travel. Can we just come out and say look at us we travel in time?" Carl went on; but writing a book about these dire issues may just work."

"Sure it would, she responded, it would not take us long to describe all the monstrous things we have witnessed firsthand in the last few days, added with what we have found in our research we could lay it out in simple terms. So simple that even the powers that be can understand it."

I was laughing, "sure thing Sandra, If this book is going to tell people about all of the apocalyptic doom we witnessed we should call the book "Gone with the Wind." Na I think that name has been taken. We can write it under a fictitious name, how about Nom de plume? Wait I think they beat us to that name too." I was still grinning as I said this.

Carl cracked up "I know a Can-Can dancer in 1901 Paris named Nom de plume, now that woman is one great story by herself. I drop in to visit with Nom often; I get a real kick out of her."

Once again all Sandra and I could do is look at each other, damn that Carl, we never know if he is putting us on or not. A Can-Can dancer named Nom de Plume?

It sounds so crazy but it sounds so much like Carl. Sandra looked at me and said *"Why the hell not?"* Carl sat there looking at us with that damn grin on his face.

"Sandra I think writing a book is a great idea. How do you want to go about doing this? Knowing you I know there has to be a plan hatching in that clever mind of yours, Sandra you always amaze me.

What's the plan Sandra, Carl asked. I am sure it is gonna be great."

Say What?
Chapter 30

"But of course I have a plan Carl, I don't leave home without one, she giggled. What we saw in the 20 minutes after we left the space station would be enough material for a great start on any book. We just need to fill in the blanks, with the computer that's easy enough to do.

We can zap up to 2018 and get it published through a publishing agency. I have a friend who had his book published by a company named "Lulu"; he said they were easy to work with, so we will check them out first."

"Oh, by the way Brian as far as the name, Gone with the Wind having been snapped up, frankly I don't give a damn." She had a twinkle in her eyes as she said this. That statement had us all laughing.

"If we did write down all the things we witnessed first hand, starting with the nuclear tests on up though our visit to the dead zone, would anyone believe what we have seen? Damn, I'm not even sure I believe it and it was all right in front of me. Hey world, we watched western states burning down. Saw miles of plastic waste floating in the Pacific; we sat a few feet over a dead zone. I mean will people believe our book or not?" Sandra asked.

"You know what I said before about nobody having any idea we can travel in time, well boys and girls I think that can work to our advantage. We will write a Science Fiction book about Time Travelers and the adventures they have in time and what they see. Best part is we can come right out and tell people, look at us, we travel in time, and no one will believe us. We don't have to change anything, just write down what we have seen since you two guys moved in to the time dome till now. So what do you guys think?"

"Carl that idea is beautiful, said Sandra and it is so simple. All we have to do is write down what we have actually seen and found out from our research, it will be totally factual and it will be real."

"I have another thought said Carl, let's write the book from Brian's point of view. Here's a guy from 1974 being slapped in the face with the reality of 2017. He is seeing these things for the first time. These are things you and I have become accustomed to Sandra and it's all new to him. It's perfect, hell we can even use Time Traveling in the title. How about Time Traveling Adventures or something along those lines?"

"Carl that is a very interesting point of view to write in, said Sandra. Someone from 1974 seeing this mess for the first time is a great place to be coming from. And you are right about writing only about what we have seen to this point. One other thing, we have to kind of zero in on is one particular issue and stay focused on that."

"Plastic is a good place to start. We will have to bring up Global warming, but that subject would take up its own book. It would mean a lot more trips to places and things I would rather not see right now, so details about global warming is on the back burner for awhile. We will get into that when we finish this book. After all we have plenty of time." Sandra looked at us, her green eyes shined.

"I feel good about writing a book from the point of view of a time traveler from 1974; it is so unbelievable I think we can get away with it." I said.

"Man if this book sells, I will have to buy a corduroy sports coat with leather patches on the elbows, oh and a pipe. All famous authors have to smoke a pipe. I read that in the famous author handbook, page 6 rule number 14." I said with a big grin.

"I have to be ready for the talk shows; I can't wait to be on the Johnnie Carson show, wow the thrill of meeting Ed McMahon, dreams do come true." I was trying to keep a straight face as I said this but I was not doing very well.

"Brian I hate to break the bad news to you but by the time this book is published Johnnie Carson is long dead, and you can get busted for what you smoke in your pipe.

Talk shows? Really Brian, wait till 2016, there are a zillion talk shows, both morning talk shows and late night talk shows."

"Somehow I can't see you hanging out chit chatting with the gang at "Good Morning America" or having coffee with Kelly. It's a good idea and all but I can't see it happening, what do you think Carl?" Sandra asked.

"Sandra I have not watched TV in years, and then I watched very few shows. All in all I didn't like it very much and I was not impressed. I have no idea what a talk show is, but it sounds horrible, people turn on a TV program to watch other people talk? Sounds kind of dull.

I see people talking everywhere I go. What happened to Bugs Bunny cartoons and the Three Stooges in the morning? Hell I'm in shock that "I Love Lucy" is still on television."

"The way I see it Sandra if Brian wants to be on talk shows it sounds cool to me. Brian is a good talker; he speaks in complete sentences and almost never says the word duh!" That statement cracked us all up.

"All famous authors smoke a pipe Brian? Did William Shakespeare smoke a pipe?" Sandra questioned.

"Hey Sandra, I read some of his writing he had to be smoking something." I answered. She laughs.

"Being a Time traveler is up there with the Easter Bunny and the Boogie Man, stated Carl. Nobody is going to believe us. That is the way it is with Time Travel, you will see. Let's get back to how we are going to write this book and what we are going to say."

"It's such a nice day and the dome is open, let's go outside and talk about our book, okay?" We both said, "Good idea Carl."

"Let go out and sit by the pool, Sandra said, the picnic table is a good place to talk. Oh boy writing a book is going to be so much fun. The Game goes on and for the first time since we started playing, I think we can win. I have to crack up thinking that three Time Travelers might change the world by writing a science fiction book about traveling in time."

"You are so right Carl; nobody will believe we really travel in time. I just hope they believe what we tell them in our book." Sandra remarked.

"Sandra you are right, this is going to be tons of fun, Carl said. Come on, let's go outside and plot, I love plotting." We got up and walked outside, into the fresh North Carolina breeze.

As we walked we continued to talk.

"I love the idea about naming the book something about Time Traveling Adventures, seeing how we are going to be writing from Brian's point of view, we should get that into the title somehow. How about the 1974 time traveler's adventures," asked Sandra?

"Na, think about it Sandra, what is Brian, besides being a mess, they both laughed, he's a surfer, who travels in time and has fun and adventures so let's zero in on that. What do you think about Adventures of a Time Traveling Surfer?" He asked.

"You know what else Brian is Carl? He is a Hippie, maybe the very last Hippie left. We should work that into the name too. I got it Sandra said, check this out;

"The Continuing Adventures of a Time Traveling Hippie Surfer."

"I love it we are going to write a science fiction book about three Time Travelers and call it "The Continuing Adventures of a Time Traveling Hippie Surfer." That is such a cool name, it is so off the wall this could work." said Carl.

We sat down at the picnic table, Carl and Sandra sat across from me. Poe laid down in the shade under the table. I could hear Sandra and Carl talking, but I was not paying any attention to them.

I could not help thinking; every day in my life is stranger then the day before.

We are going to write and publish a book about all the horrible things we have witnessed firsthand in the last few days of our Time Traveling.

Damn I wonder if anyone will read this book and if they do, will they get off their ass and get involved with cleaning up the huge mess humans have made out of the world.

Carl said something earlier about little steps, like bend down, pick it up. It has to start someplace, think about it what choice do you really have?

This Game is forever. Maybe the people will stand up and say enough. Only time will tell.

Sandra, Carl and I have lots and lots of time.

I could hear The Stones starting to play the song "Time is on my side." Man I love this song, it was playing when I found the Dome of Time.

"Time is on my side yes it is, time, time, time is on my side, oh yes it is."

I had to wonder though, after everything I have seen and heard in the last few days, how much time the rest of the world really has left.

The end.... Maybe?

About the Author

Brian was born in New York City, into a military family and started traveling around the U.S. and Europe almost immediately.

He began surfing in Honolulu in 1962 and never stopped. Working as a Merchant Seaman he continued to travel the world.

Surfing is still his passion.

Brian writes because he has stories to tell.